Kelly Hunter has always had a weakness for fairy tales, fantasy worlds and losing herself in a good book. She has two children, avoids cooking and cleaning and, despite the best efforts of her family, is no sports fan. Kelly *is*, however, a keen gardener, and has a fondness for roses. Kelly was born in Australia and has travelled extensively. Although she enjoys living and working in different parts of the world, she still calls Australia home.

Also by Kelly Hunter

Claimed by a King miniseries

Shock Heir for the Crown Prince

And look out for the next book
Convenient Bride for the King
Available March 2018

Discover more at millsandboon.co.uk

SHOCK HEIR
FOR THE
CROWN PRINCE

BY
KELLY HUNTER

MILLS & BOON

First Published in Great Britain 2018
by Mills & Boon, an imprint of HarperCollins*Publishers*
1 London Bridge Street, London, SE1 9GF

ISBN: 978-0-263-07539-7

MIX
Paper from
responsible sources
FSC **FSC® C007454**

This book is produced from independently certified FSC™ paper
to ensure responsible forest management.
For more information visit www.harpercollins.co.uk/green.

Printed and bound in Great Britain
by CPI Group (UK) Ltd, Croydon, CR0 4YY

PROLOGUE

CASIMIR, CROWN PRINCE OF BYZENMAACH, woke with a woman on his mind and an ache in his loins. He rolled onto his back, and let out a groan when the heavy cotton sheet rubbed against him in just the right way to make his hips move again, and then again. Not this again. Not her again—it was the third time this week.

He wasn't impressed.

It took longer than usual to shove those wayward memories of lovemaking aside and roll out of bed. Naked, he padded across age-old silk carpets towards the door that led to the parapet that led to the bathhouse—a domed white marble indulgence that would have found favour with the gladiators of Rome.

Cool air hit his skin the minute he opened the huge double doors, and if he hadn't been fully awake before, he was now. Summer was in full swing in Byzenmaach but here in the snow-capped northern mountains the mornings still held the edge of winter on them and always would. He suffered it because he liked the cool lick of ice on his skin and because it made that moment when he entered the hot pool that much sweeter.

Nothing could ease the tension in his body and clear his mind faster than spending five minutes beneath the pounding man-made waterfall at the far edge of the hot

pool and then another five immersed in the still and silent water at the other end of it. Access to the bathhouse
was one of the main reasons he'd made Byzenmaach's
remote winter fortress his permanent home.

Hedonist. He'd never deny the label. Pleasure-seeking
was an integral part of his nature.

It wasn't all he was.

The woman on his mind—Ana—had been a mistake,
a youthful indiscretion, a hedonistic folly, and every so
often she haunted him. She'd been a student of languages,
living in Geneva. He'd been on his way home from delegate talks and bored. The bar where they'd first met had
been called the Barrel and Fawn.

Who remembered details like that seven years after
the encounter?

The walkway to the bathhouse was open to the air on
one side, courtesy of a waist-high stone wall and colon-
nade arches. The view that greeted him stretched out over
the valley below and still managed to impress, no matter
how many times he saw it. Once winter hit he'd take the
long way round through the palace, but until then he'd
enjoy the caress of cool mountain air on his skin. Perhaps it would cool his morning ardour.

It didn't.

Why was it that seven years after the affair, Anastasia Douglas was still his go-to memory when his body
sought release?

Why did he remember the way she took her morning
coffee when he had hundreds, if not thousands, of more
important memories to recall?

Double shot, black, with one sugar, and hot enough
to burn.

Her hair, a tousled black cloud that framed exquisite
bone structure as she purred her contentment and blew

on the steaming black liquid to cool it before setting it to her lips.

He hadn't been the only hedonist in their short-lived relationship. The things she could do with her mouth...

He shivered and it wasn't just because of the cool dawn air.

There'd been something in the air, in the water, on the night he'd met her. Something that had him acting with greater than usual abandon. He'd made the first move, used every bit of charm in his arsenal, and before the night was through they'd ended up naked in her tiny student apartment on the outskirts of the city. He'd stayed the night and instead of leaving the next morning he'd stayed four more nights, turning his back on everything but her. Learning her. Loving her. Ramming into her life and meeting no resistance.

He'd monopolised her nights and infiltrated her days.

They'd lain on the grass in a tiny gated park with his face to the sun and Ana's head on his hip as she read Russian poetry to him in flawless Russian and then again in English. She'd been equally fluent in both languages, or so she'd said—courtesy of her Russian mother and English father—but the results of her translations had been confusing.

Russian poetry was never meant to be read in English, she'd said, which had begged the question as to why she was attempting the impossible in the first place.

She wanted to be an interpreter, she'd said. Maybe for the European Parliament, maybe for the United Nations Secretariat, and to do that she had to be the best of the best. She was practising.

She'd shared her goals and ambitions, her body and her home.

He'd shared next to nothing.

She hadn't known she was talking to the Crown Prince of Byzenmaach, with his impeccable lineage, private planes and castles carved into the side of mountains.

He hadn't told her he was Casimir, dutiful son and heir to the throne, student of politics since he was old enough to stand at his father's knee and listen.

For four days and five nights he hadn't been Casimir, with his dead mother and sister, an ailing father and responsibilities he hadn't been ready for. She'd called him Cas, just Cas, and the freedom to *be* Just Cas had been liberating.

Maybe *that* was why he kept remembering Anastasia Douglas every so often. Her breathy cries and the softness of her skin, the way she'd wrapped around him... maybe he equated her with freedom, or the illusion of freedom. Maybe his longing to choose his own path sat in his subconscious like a burr, never mind that he'd come to terms with his royal responsibilities long ago.

The waters of the bath glinted deep blue and silver in the weak light of morning. Steam spiralled towards the high domed ceiling, and the caress of water on his feet as he took that first step down into the pool made him groan his pleasure.

He liked that the water temperature was almost too hot to bear.

Same way Ana had liked her coffee.

He took another step into the pool and then another, the water now lapping at his thighs, his erection in no way deflated by the sensory experience of cold air followed by the lick of hot water.

Soon he would propose to Princess Moriana from the neighbouring monarchy of Arun. Moriana was smart, educated, well versed in affairs of state and extremely well connected. It wasn't a love match but he wouldn't regret the union. Moriana would be good for him and for Byzenmaach. He *knew* this.

Moriana, not Anastasia.

He tried to turn his thoughts towards his intended, but it was no use. Ana won.

Ana always won.

Turning on his heel, he stepped back out of the pool and headed for the shower, half hidden in the marble recesses beside the far door. He turned the taps, adjusted the heat and let fat water droplets fall to the floor before stepping beneath them. He reached for the body oil rather than the soap and took himself in hand.

Maybe he should find out what Anastasia Douglas was doing these days as a way of getting her out of his head. Maybe she'd be married now and wildly content with her husband and two point three children. Unavailable, unobtainable. No longer the woman who'd loved Cas, just Cas, and wished him happiness.

New memories, lesser ones, to replace the memories that haunted him still. Ana, sated and smiling, all long limbs, alabaster skin and silky black hair that a man could lose his fist in. Ana on her knees for him while he muttered words like *please* and *more* on more than one occasion. Ana, with her open sensuality that had ignited his.

No pressure, no reputation to uphold, no expectations and no demands. Pleasure for pleasure's sake. Quick, clever hands and lips that dragged in all the right places. Tumbling words of fire and passion that his soul understood, even if the actual words had been a mystery to him.

Surely, in his mind, if nowhere else, he could have this.

Closing his eyes and turning his face upwards into the water, he let the memories come.

CHAPTER ONE

'YOUR HIGHNESS, A moment of your time.'

Casimir looked up from the papers on his desk and nodded for Rudolpho to enter. The king's chief advisor looked more careworn than usual but that was only to be expected given that his king, Casimir's father, was dying. Loyal to a fault, Rudolpho had found the transfer of power from Leonidas to Casimir an unpalatable process. Crown Prince or not, Rudolpho was first and foremost the king's man.

And he didn't always like the changes Casimir was insisting on.

Soon Casimir would have to leave his winter fortress and take up permanent residence in the palace in the capital. Soon he would no longer have to bear witness to his father's relentless march towards death. He and his father weren't close. A big part of him loathed the man, and always would. Another part pitied him. And then there was a tiny sliver of Casimir's soul that craved the man's approval.

It wasn't like Rudolpho to hang back in doorways, but the older man still hadn't entered the room and his stance was stiffer than usual. Something was amiss. 'What news of my father?' he asked.

'Your father had a comfortable evening. Morphine

helps. He's sleeping now.' Rudolpho approached the desk, his gaze roving over the neat stacks of paperwork to either side of Casimir's laptop. 'You need to delegate some of this workload.'

'I intend to. Just as soon as I understand exactly what it is I'm delegating.' Some of these duties were new to him. Not many, but some, and Casimir was nothing if not thorough. 'I thought you left the palace hours ago.' Casimir let his raised eyebrow ask the obvious question.

If the king was resting comfortably and Rudolpho had a rare evening off, what was he doing here?

Rudolpho set a yellow courier's envelope on the desk as if he couldn't wait for it to leave his hand. 'The report you ordered on Anastasia Douglas came in. I took the liberty of opening it.'

'You open everything.' Nothing unusual about that.

'Not every report I glance through threatens my ability to breathe. Did you know?'

The older man's voice had taken on a hard, precise edge, with an undertone of something Casimir couldn't quite place. Fear? Despair? Maybe it was disappointment. 'Know what?'

'I'll be in my office,' Rudolpho said, and stalked away, his spine one ramrod line of displeasure.

Disappointment it was. Casimir eyed the offending envelope with deep suspicion before reaching for it.

New memories to replace the old, he reminded himself grimly. Closure, rather than curiosity. Nothing to worry about. He'd asked for this.

So why did his hand tremble ever so slightly as he reached in and withdrew the contents of the envelope?

There were photos, lots of photos, and the topmost image was a close-up of Ana's face. A heart-shaped face, wide of brow and pointy of chin, with eyes to drown in and lips that promised heaven. Strong, shapely eyebrows and lashes, thick and black, made the cerulean blue of her eyes all the more arresting. In this picture her hair had been scraped back into a careless ponytail. In the next photo it framed her face in sultry waves that curled around her neck and shoulders. It was a face to stop a man's breath. Casimir put a hand to *his* face and rubbed hard before turning to the next photograph.

So she'd grown into her beauty. No surprises there.

The next shot was a full-body take of Ana walking up a set of wide outdoor steps—rushing up them most likely, because her body was a study in motion. Slender legs and rounded curves and, again, that loose mane of ebony hair. She wore a dark grey corporate skirt and jacket and had a black satchel slung over her left shoulder. Two more photos showed similar variations on a corporate theme.

The next photo showed her in jeans and a pink short-sleeved T-shirt, standing outside school gates with a young schoolgirl by her side. The photographer had caught them from the rear, as Ana adjusted the shoulder strap of the girl's backpack. So she was a mother now—good for her. Hopefully she had a husband to love and a solid family life. Casimir looked to her hand to see if she wore a wedding ring but the photo didn't allow for that level of detail.

The next shot was a formal school photo of the child.

At which point the world as Casimir knew it simply stopped.

There was no sound. No air.

Grey threatened the edges of his sight.

No.

Yes.

Casimir had had a sister once. For seven years he'd

had a sister three years younger than he was. And then the rebels to the north had taken her and when his father hadn't agreed to their demands they'd killed her and sent back pieces to prove it.

His mother had never recovered. She'd taken her own life a year later to the day, leaving her husband and her son to carry on alone.

They didn't talk about it, Cas and his father. They never had and probably never would. Therapists had been out of the question—too much potential for exploitation to ever let someone inside the young Prince of Byzenmaach's head, so Cas had survived as best he could.

The pictures of his mother and sister remained prominent in the palace—a permanent reminder of failure, loss and grief. One of the first things he'd do as king would be to remove them to a rarely used dining room and shut the door on them.

Such a small and petty command for a new monarch to give.

He couldn't look away from the picture of the girl. The cloud of unruly black hair, the cowlick at the child's temple, the aristocratic blade of her nose.

Those eyes.

He put his hands to his own eyes and rubbed, but the picture was still there.

There would be no getting rid of this.

More pictures followed and each one brought with it a barrage of conflicting emotions because from a distance the kid could be any young girl, but up close…up close, and especially around the eyes—the hawkish, tawny-gold colour of her eyes…

The photo of her twirling in the garden, arms outstretched as if to catch the dust motes in the air…

Heaven help him, he was ten years old again, only

this time he hadn't left his sister alone in the garden to go and get a jar to catch the praying mantis in, and when he came back she hadn't been gone.

Taken.

Kidnapped.

And never coming back.

Weakness didn't sit well on him but he'd rather cut his own eyes out than look at another photo of Anastasia Douglas's daughter. Cas closed his eyes and concentrated on the formerly simple act of breathing.

The clink of glasses and a bottle thudding down on the table prevented him from doing either. Rudolpho was back, and with him a glass and a bottle of Royal Vault brandy. Age spots and veins stood out on the older man's hands as he poured generously and pushed the glass into Casimir's hand.

'I don't know the royal protocol for this,' Rudolpho said gruffly. 'But drink. You're white.'

'She's… It's…' Cas took a steadying breath. 'It's not her.'

'No. It's not her,' Rudolpho said evenly. 'But the likeness is uncanny. How far did you get?'

Wordlessly, Casimir picked up the photo of the child in the garden. Rudolpho winced.

'Summarise,' Casimir said.

Rudolpho sighed and stared momentarily at the brandy. Casimir gestured for him to have one and succeeded only in offending the man. Rudolpho was a product of an earlier era and would no more sit and drink with Casimir, Crown Prince, than fly. It wasn't done. It breached a thousand protocols. 'The child is six years old and has a British birth certificate, courtesy of her being born at the Portland Hospital in London and her mother's chosen nationality.'

Now it was Casimir's turn to wince at the thought of a child of Byzenmaach claiming a foreign nationality.

'The mother is Anastasia Victoria Douglas,' Rudolpho continued. 'Twenty-six years of age. Marital status: single. Occupation: interpreter for the European Parliament and the United Nations Secretariat. Currently residing in Geneva, where most of her work is.'

'And the father?' He had to ask. He already knew.

'Father unknown.'

So.

Casimir, future king of Byzenmaach, had an illegitimate six-year-old daughter. A daughter who was the spitting image of his long-dead sister.

'Your name isn't on the birth certificate,' Rudolpho pointed out quietly. 'Maybe the child's *not* yours. Maybe Anastasia Douglas doesn't *know* who the father is.'

Cas silently rifled through the photos for the headshot of the girl in school uniform and held it up.

Rudolpho could barely bring himself to glance at it. 'Maybe the mother has a weakness for amber-eyed men. My point being that the girl's mother hasn't contacted you in seven years. She hasn't asked you for anything, least of all acknowledgement. She provides amply for the child. The girl has a roof over her head, good schooling, loving grandparents. The child is intelligent. She won't lack for life choices.'

'Are you suggesting I don't acknowledge her?'

Rudolpho stayed silent.

'That's your counsel?'

'Or you could bring her here,' Rudolpho said finally. 'And do your best to protect her.'

Temper soared. 'You think I can't?' Never mind that Casimir had been the one to leave his sister unprotected in the first place. 'You think I'm like *him*?'

'I think…' Rudolpho paused, as if choosing his words carefully. 'I think this innocent bastard child looks like your sister reincarnated. She'd be a target for your enemies from the outset. Front page fodder for the press.'

Silence fell again, the deeply unsettling kind.

'This stays between us for now,' Casimir said finally.

Rudolpho met his gaze. 'It can stay between us for ever, if that is your wish.'

Could he do it? Casimir glanced at the pictures strewn across his desk. Could he really shut her out the way he'd shut out all memory of his seven-year-old sister and too-weak-for-this-world mother? Pack all the pictures away and never look back?

Could he really continue on as if the girl simply didn't exist?

The child was his blood. *His* responsibility. His to protect. 'What's her name?' he asked gruffly.

'Your Highness, the less you know the easier it'll be to—

'What's her name?'

'Sophia.' Rudolpho sounded defeated. 'Sophia Alexandra Douglas.'

A fitting name for the daughter of a king.

Had she known? Had Anastasia Douglas known who she was getting in bed with?

'Your Highness—'

'Enough!' Whatever it was, he didn't want to hear it.

'Your Highness, *please*. Sleep on this. Think carefully before you expose the child to Byzenmaach, because there's no coming back from that. They'll take her and shape her into whatever they most desire, and you'll have to protect her from that too.'

'The way my father never did for me?' Casimir asked, silky-soft and deadly.

Rudolpho remained silent. Never would he speak ill of the king he'd served for over forty years.

'Are you asking if I can accept this child as a person in her own right—with strengths and flaws of her own making? Can I protect her from the expectations of others? Do I know how to be a father to a child who carries the expectations of a nation on her shoulders? Is that your *concern*?'

Rudolpho said nothing.

'I *was* that child,' he grated. 'Who better to defend her exploitation than me?'

Casimir scowled and reached for his drink again. He knew exactly what his father would do with this information, and it would be as Rudolpho said. Use the girl to shore up a nation's hope until legitimate heirs were produced, then cast her aside because she no longer fitted in the Byzenmaach monarch's perfect world. She wouldn't have it easy here. No child of Byzenmaach ever did.

The desk, this room and everything in it stank of duty and the weight that came with it. 'You really think a part of me doesn't realise that the kindest thing I can do for both of them is to leave them alone?'

All that, and still…

'She's mine,' he said. '*My* child. *My* blood. My responsibility.'

The bottom line in all of this.

And yet.

And yet…

Could he really expose the child to the dangers that awaited her here in Byzenmaach?

'There's one more thing.' Rudolpho eyed him warily. 'We weren't the only ones watching them. Anastasia Douglas and her daughter were already under surveillance. There was a team on the house, and another in place at the girl's school. As far as we could ascertain, their focus was the girl rather than the mother.'

Dread turned his skin cold and clammy. 'Who were they?'

'We don't know. They disappeared before we could deal with them. They're good.'

Not good.

'I've ordered a covert security team to watch and wait for additional orders,' said Rudolpho. 'I don't think it wise to involve your father in any decision-making at this point.'

His father only had days to live. That was what Rudolpho meant. 'I'll handle it.'

'If you need additional counsel—'

Casimir smiled bleakly. 'I don't.'

CHAPTER TWO

ANASTASIA DOUGLAS DIDN'T usually attend black-tie fund-raising events at the director of the United Nations Secretariat's request. She was a lowly interpreter, one of many, even if she did have a reputation for being extremely good at what she did. She commanded five languages instead of the average three and was conversationally fluent in half a dozen more. She could navigate diplomatic circles with ease, courtesy of the training she'd received at her Russian diplomat mother's knee. She had an intimate understanding of world politics, and enough corporate mediation experience to be of use when conversation got heated. All good things for a career interpreter's toolkit.

It still didn't explain why she was here in Geneva's fading Museum of Art and History, talking black tulips with the Minister for Transport's wife. The ticket would be held for her at the door, the director had said. It was important for her to be there, he'd said. Someone wanted to meet her in person, in advance of securing her services.

It would help mightily, Ana thought grimly, if she knew who that person was.

Twenty more minutes and Ana would cut her losses and make her exit. She was drawing enough unwanted attention as it was—possibly because she'd put her hair up and was wearing the simple black gown her mother had bought her for Christmas. It had a discreet boat neckline, no sleeves, and clung to her curves like a lover's hand. Very little skin was showing. The dress was more than appropriate for such an event, and yet...

It didn't matter that she never particularly wanted to draw the male gaze, she drew it regardless. And the female gaze and the gaze of the security guard stationed at the door. Sex appeal, mystery, an air of worldliness—whatever it was, people always stared. Some envious, some dazzled, others covetous. No one was ever neutral around her.

When Ana had fallen pregnant at nineteen, with barely any knowledge of the father and no way to contact him again, her mother had been horrified. All those plans for Ana to make a powerfully advantageous marriage, gone. All Ana's formidable allure spent on a man who didn't want her.

Only he had wanted her.

For one glorious week Ana had been the centre of a laughing, passionate, attentive man's world and she'd gloried in it. He'd smiled at her in a bar and she'd felt the warmth of it all the way to her toes. He'd put a hand to the small of her back and held the door open for her on their way out and she'd stumbled beneath the heat of it all.

Clumsy Ana, when she'd never been clumsy before. All lit up at the touch of his hand.

So young. So utterly confident that the pulsing connection between them would last for ever. For one unforgettable week she'd found heaven here on earth. And then he'd left without a word, no farewell and no forwarding address.

He's married, nothing surer, her mother had said.

You don't have to have this baby, she'd said months

later. *You could move on with your life. Continue with your study plans.*

Wise words from a woman Ana had always respected, only Ana had never quite been able to turn that stolen week into nothing. Never quite been able to wipe it from her consciousness.

She'd been nine months pregnant before she'd even figured out who Cas, *her* Cas, was. Not married. Not some feckless con man who'd needed a place to stay for a week.

He'd been the Crown Prince of Byzenmaach.

She'd woven that information into something she could live with; of course she had.

He hadn't left her because he wanted to; he'd left her because duty to his crown demanded it. His father had forbidden it, and he'd fought for her, hard, but been overruled. He'd spent weeks in a dungeon, clamouring to get out and return to her. *Yeah.* Ana smiled ruefully. That last fantasy had always been a favourite.

Far better than the bitter knowledge that she simply hadn't been a suitable choice for him and that he'd known it from the start and chosen to love her and leave her regardless.

She hadn't got in touch.

The Transport Minister's wife had exhausted the topic of tulips. By mutual consent they headed towards a larger circle of people, allowing Ana to drift away, towards a Grecian bust, champagne glass in hand. She rarely drank, although at an event such as this she would often take a glass of whatever they were offering. She liked to think it made her fit in.

The sculpture wasn't the most impressive one in the room but studying it served the purpose of separating her from the crowd. She stood alone. Approachable. Any potential employer could introduce themselves now, in private, assuming they wanted to. If they didn't, not a problem. She *had* enough work lined up to keep her and Sophia living comfortably for quite some time.

No one could accuse her of not giving her daughter a good start in life.

She felt the presence of someone at her side before she saw them. The movement of air, a dark shape in her peripheral vision. She turned to look at him, and felt the bottom drop out of her world.

She'd have known him anywhere, never mind that it had been years since she'd seen him last. She'd mapped that face with her lips and fingertips, and left not one inch of his body unexplored. Broad of shoulder and long of leg, his shoes were black and shiny and his shirt was snowy white beneath his black suit. His hands were in the pockets of his trousers, stretching the fabric taut across his abdomen and the top of his thighs.

Hurriedly, she turned her attention back to the Grecian bust, giving it far more attention than it deserved. Her palms felt suddenly slick and she longed to wipe them down the sides of her gown. Instead she wrapped both hands around her glass and tried to ignore the thunderous beating of her heart.

She hadn't forgotten him, no, she could never do that. She woke to a living, breathing reminder of him every morning and fed her cheese on toast.

'Hello, Ana,' he said quietly.

'Cas.'

'Been a while,' he said.

'Yes.'

'You're looking well. A little pale. Must be all that working indoors.'

'You know where I work?'

'I had you investigated.'

'Oh.' *Stay cool, Ana.* There was still a chance he didn't know about Sophia. 'Why?'

He smiled grimly and shook his head. Shrugging those powerful shoulders as if to say he didn't understand it either. 'In truth—which is more than you deserve—my father is dying and I need to marry soon. The woman my country has in mind for me is a princess from a neighbouring principality. We've been informally promised to each other since we were nine years old and I wanted to do right by her before making it official. I wanted to put you—and the week we once shared—out of my mind for good.'

'That's right. You're the Crown Prince of Byzenmaach.' She smiled, because she knew the power in her smile. *'In truth*, that was something I deserved to know all those years ago, when you graced my bed. Don't you think?'

Now it was Casimir's turn to study the Grecian bust. 'I don't disagree,' he offered finally.

She looked at his proud profile and wondered for the umpteenth time why he'd done it. Spent the week with her, pretending to be someone he was not. Was his life really that bad that he'd needed to escape it? Or had he too been blindsided by attraction?

'A lot of my choices would have been different had I known who you really were,' she said.

'They always are,' he replied somewhat grimly.

'So you had me investigated.' Carefully, she picked up the earlier thread of their conversation. 'How is that supposed to help put me out of your mind for good?'

'You were supposed to have developed flaws.'

'What kind of flaws?'

'Any kind at all.'

'Should I have lost teeth and grown warts?'

'Yes.' The glimmer of a smile chased the shadows from his eyes, but only for a moment. 'You were supposed to have moved on.'

'I *have* moved on. We had a good time. It's done.'

'You're the mother of my child,' he countered flatly.

Right. That.

As for Ana's response, she'd prepared for this day. She had words in place in at least five languages.

'You're wrong.' Those were the first words in her arsenal. She glanced up to see how he'd taken them. Not well, if his fierce and unforgiving glare was anything to go by.

'Do I need to order a DNA test for the child?' he enquired silkily. 'Because I will if I have to. I will regardless, so let's move past denial. We both know she's mine.'

If denial wasn't working, try reason. 'Walk away, Your Highness. You don't have to be here.'

'You say that as if it's an option.' He kept his voice low but anger ran like a river beneath his words. 'It's not.'

'Marry your princess, produce an heir to your throne and forget about me and mine. It *is* an option.' She turned imploring eyes on him. 'I'm well set up. I can provide for my daughter. You *don't* have to be here.'

'Does she ask about her father?'

Ana squared her shoulders and told it like it was. She'd tackled that question back when Sophia had been four years old. Not Ana's finest moment. But the lie had fallen from her lips and there was no taking it back. 'I told her you were dead. No one knows who Sophia's father is. *No one.* Not even my parents.'

'You say that as if it's something to be proud of.'

'Isn't it?' she said haughtily. 'Think of it as protection rather than oversight, and maybe you'll see where I'm coming from.'

His lips tightened.

'I found out who you were purely by chance.' Ana had the advantage so she pressed it. 'I was nine months pregnant at the time, you were long gone and I'd already made the decision to raise my baby alone. I saw your picture in a Middle Eastern newspaper one of my mother's guests had left behind. Suddenly your joy in the little everyday things we did made so much more sense. As did your disappearing act at the end.'

Needing distance, she walked around the statue, putting it between them even as their gazes stayed locked. 'I researched you; how could I not? I read about your sister's death and your mother's suicide. Your father stood tall throughout.' Ana badly wanted to reach out and run her fingers over the cold, smooth marble, but it wasn't allowed. 'I remember looking at the pictures of him and thinking how stalwart he was. The widower king who held it together, with you at his side…ten years old and so determined not to disappoint. You were your country's last hope. You still are.'

She'd watched him walk away once before; she could do it again. 'I'll never know why you took up with me in the first place, but you left me behind for a reason, maybe for a whole lot of reasons. So I left your name off my daughter's birth certificate for a reason too.' She stared at him, willing him to understand. 'Go home, Your Highness. I've got this.'

'Come with me,' he offered gruffly, his gaze never leaving hers. 'Bring her.'

This wasn't how the conversation ever went in her imagination. In her imagination he walked away, relieved by her silence. 'You haven't heard a word I said.'

'On the contrary, I'm listening very carefully. You seem to know broadly what's at stake, which makes this meeting easier than expected. I discovered my daughter's existence three days ago. I want to meet her.'

'No.' She took a careful step left, partially obscuring him from her line of sight. 'That's not advisable.'

He tilted his head, the better to keep her in view. 'It wasn't a request. I have a jet waiting and a security team in place outside your house, awaiting orders.' The smile he sent her was a worn and bitter thing. 'I'm sorry, Ana. I had hoped for a more leisurely approach but circumstances beyond my control are against it. I need you and Sophia in Byzenmaach.'

'No.'

'For your own protection, as well as mine,' he said. 'Perhaps it's you who needs to listen a little more carefully. Because it's not a request.'

There were other ways he could have gone about getting access to the child. Official, less invasive ways but all of them took time and time was something Casimir didn't have. He'd carved out the hours and minutes it took to come here to collect them, and even gaining that amount of freedom had been harder than carving granite with bare hands. He didn't have time to ease himself slowly into Ana and his daughter's life.

They had to come to him.

'My car is out front,' he said.

'Mine is in the car park.'

And if she thought he would allow her to drive it back to her house, she was mistaken. 'Someone will make sure your vehicle is returned to your apartment.'

'I need to go to the ladies' room,' she said next, glancing around as if weighing her options.

'By all means.' He nodded towards the severely

dressed woman who stood by the stairway, her eyes sharply trained on them. 'Katya will escort you.'

Ana swayed suddenly and he stepped closer and put his hand to the small of her back to steady her. Her skin was warm beneath the thin fabric of her dress and her breath hitched. It was all he could do to stop from lowering his head to the curve of her neck and breathing her in. Desire hit him, stronger than the desire he'd felt for her all those years ago. A staggering certainty that this woman would always be the woman he measured all others against. 'Are you afraid of me?'

She glanced at him and their gazes caught and held. She feared him now, this woman who'd once offered him all that she had to give. He could feel it in the slight trembling beneath his hand.

'I'm afraid of what you might take from me, yes.' Her quietly contained reply made honesty seem like strength.

'Perhaps I'll share,' he muttered as he took her drink and gave it to a passing waiter. 'Right now my father is ill, I need to return to Byzenmaach and I don't have time to waste. I could have sent strangers to collect you, but I thought you might prefer a familiar face.'

He hadn't wanted her or their daughter to feel the terror of abduction.

He steered her towards the exit and Katya fell silently into step beside them. Another security type stood waiting by the door to the museum, holding Ana's coat over one arm. Ana faltered when she saw him and Casimir slowed his steps to match.

'Cas, please. I don't want this.' She looked at him imploringly and put her hand on his sleeve to hold him back. 'I know what will happen once you claim her. She'll be in the spotlight. A target for those who oppose you. I don't want her to be a target. I want to keep my daughter safe.'

It had been seven years since they'd breathed the same air, but her effect on him was as potent as he remembered. He wanted to touch and he wanted to take. Sip at her lips and drive them both mad, until memories became their reality.

'That's what I'm trying to do. On my grave, Anastasia. I will keep you and your daughter safe.'

She let him escort her out of the museum and towards the waiting car, and Casimir was grateful for her acquiescence. Approaching Anastasia in public had been a calculated risk that his security team had advised against. They'd wanted to approach her at her home. He'd wanted to make his approach while the child wasn't with her and he'd only had an evening to do it in. Easy enough for him to pull strings and arrange for her to be here this evening.

She got into the car without comment and he followed, as his bodyguards peeled away, one towards another vehicle, the other sliding into the front seat beside the driver. He had a team of eight in place for the pickup. Four here and four more at Ana's house. Overkill, but he was taking no chances. He could see the trembling of Ana's hands as she clenched them together in her lap. The trembling didn't stop, so with a shaky huff of breath she shoved her tell-tale hands beneath her thighs and sat on them.

'Better?' he said.

'Interpreter training didn't encompass fearlessness in the face of abduction.'

'You're doing very well.'

Ana cut short what might have been a bitter laugh and looked out of the window as the museum swept from view. He let her be, more content with the darkness of the car and the silence, and her presence, than he had any right to be.

'What's wrong with your father?' she asked finally.

'Cancer.'

'How long does he have left?'

'Days.'

She nodded, and he appreciated her lack of false platitudes for a man she'd never met.

'Do you want Sophia to meet him?' she asked next, and it was a fair question. One he had yet to answer for himself.

'I haven't arranged it.'

'Because your father will be disappointed that you spawned a bastard child?'

'Because Sophia is the image of my sister at that age and my father is not always lucid,' he countered. 'He'll see what he wants to see rather than reality, and I would protect her from that kind of confusion.'

'And what will you see when you look at Sophia?' she asked.

'I don't know.' Truth again, and it sat uneasily on him after a lifetime of concealing his innermost thoughts and feelings. 'Ask me again in fifteen minutes.'

'Casimir, Your Highness, I'm not ready for this.'

Neither was he, but he was doing it. 'My father resides in the royal palace in Byzenmaach's capital but that's not where we're going. We're going to my private residence instead. It's a fortress under lockdown. There will be no press. No courtiers. You'll be safe there.'

'I was safe here,' she said.

'No, Anastasia. You weren't. You and Sophia were already under surveillance when we came looking for you.'

'I don't believe you.' She looked mutinous. 'We *are* safe here. Safer than we'd be with you.'

He reached into the pocket of the seat in front of him and drew out an envelope and handed it to her. 'This is all we've been able to come up with on those who have you under surveillance.' She opened the envelope and photos spilled out. 'That's the school's new contract gardener. He's a Byzenmaach national with ties to those who took my sister.'

Ana said nothing as she flipped to the next photo, but her lips tightened.

'Your new neighbours of three months. They live across the road from you. The woman is a Byzenmaach national. She's the granddaughter of the speaker for the Northern mountain tribes of Byzenmaach. He unifies them. He's also the one who ordered my sister's abduction. That or allowed it to happen. That's her real husband, by the way. He's Swiss. We don't know whether he's part of your surveillance team or not.'

Ana's hands trembled but she firmed them up fast and flicked over to the next photo. This one was of her sitting at a café with a co-worker. Her neighbour sat two tables away, reading the paper. 'So they watch. So what? They haven't done anything.'

'Yet.' He laid it out for her as plainly as he could. 'The Northern rebels are ruthless. Sophia is of royal blood and may be used against me. I'd rather have her at my side than see her in their clutches. I've already seen one show of theirs and I don't need a repeat performance.'

'Cas.' She shook her head, clearly not wanting to believe any of it. 'I can't— This isn't my life.'

But it was. 'I'm sorry, Anastasia. Had there been no other eyes on you I might have been able to leave you alone. Not saying I would have, but it was an option. That option ceased to exist the moment we identified who else we were dealing with. At that point I *had* to step in. Now that I have there's no coming back from that. Not for any of us. The world you woke up to this morning is gone.'

She said nothing.

'If it's any consolation this is an equal opportunity disaster. The world as I know it shattered too, the moment I discovered I had a daughter.'

'How very even-handed,' she said faintly.

'Isn't it. You always were fluent in understatement.' He'd always found it vaguely entertaining. 'How many languages are you fluent in now?'

'Six.'

'Your UN résumé says five.'

'They missed one.'

Not exactly reticent when it came to her skill set. Maybe that was a good thing, given the political world he was thrusting her into. 'Which one did they miss?'

'Yours.'

He blinked. Calculated the benefits of her being fluent in his native tongue and there were plenty. 'Thank God for that.'

'God has nothing to do with it. I learn fast. I was bored one day and picked up a dictionary.'

'You'll assimilate faster if you can speak the language. You may even be able to work as an interpreter for the palace.'

'Why would I want to do that? I've already achieved my workplace goals,' she snapped.

So she had. 'Will the UN allow you to work remotely?' They might. He'd not object.

'Casimir, I don't know exactly what you're thinking, but my career is here. I've worked hard to build it and I have no intention of throwing it away because you think Sophia and I would be safer in Byzenmaach. You have a problem on your Northern borders? Fix it. And then we can all get on with our lives.'

'It's really not that simple.' He'd expected resistance. Possibly not quite this much resistance, but still… He'd come prepared to bargain. To say whatever he had to say in order to get her on that plane. 'Anastasia, please. Take some leave from your work, come with me to Byzenmaach—where I need to be and where I can protect you—and let us work through this. You're right. These people may not be a threat to you or Sophia. Maybe they want to welcome you into their community with open arms and treasure you both for reasons unknown. It's possible. But right now we don't know what they want from you. What if I ask for a mere two weeks of your time? Enough time to build a case either for or against you and Sophia returning to Geneva. Right now I don't consider that an option but perhaps you can convince me otherwise. I'm not an unreasonable man. We can negotiate.'

She handed the photos and the envelope back to him and stared out of the car window by way of reply.

'The palace will provide amply for both you and Sophia. Money won't be an issue.' Possibly not the point but still worth mentioning.

'Thank you,' she grated, still not looking at him. 'Being dependent on someone else for the roof over my head, the clothes that I wear and the food in my mouth has always been one of my primary goals.'

'Irony, right?'

She cut him a look that could have shredded steel.

'Just checking. Some people wouldn't have a problem with being kept, given the circumstances.'

Although it seemed unlikely that she would be one of them and make life easier for everyone.

'Independence is hardly a character flaw,' she said. 'Try thinking of it as a strength.'

'I'd like to.' He really would. He just didn't know how much of an asset it would be when navigating the demands of royal existence.

Ana lived in an apartment just outside Geneva's UN precinct. By the time they reached it, a cold, illogical fear had begun to assail him. His daughter was in there. A daughter he'd never met, who was the image of his sister. A daughter who thought him dead.

'Ten minutes,' he said as he exited the car and leaned against the bonnet. 'Clothes, passports, belongings you can't live without. Whatever you're likely to need for your stay, bring it.'

'You're not coming in?'

'Am I invited?'

'You hijack my life and yet you stand here and ask for an invitation inside? What are you, a vampire?'

'I'm courteous.'

She laughed as if she couldn't help it, a sudden brightness in a night full of shadows and wrongdoing. 'You're everything I never wanted and can't forget,' she said. 'Presumably you've prepared for meeting your daughter as ruthlessly as you prepared for everything else.'

'Yes.'

She paused, both hands to the little blue door of her house. 'If you remember nothing else, remember this. If you hurt my daughter...if you ever make her feel less than the beautiful, innocent child she is... I will make you regret it.' Her voice was shaking and so were her hands but she turned to spear him with eyes fiercer than any eagle in his aviary. 'I will protect my child with my last breath. It's what mothers do.'

'Not in my experience.'

'Maybe you need more experience.' She turned away from him, put the key in the lock and pushed it open. 'My warning stands.'

He watched her enter, squared his shoulders and followed. He knew nothing of parenting, or of six-year-old girls, except that maybe, just maybe, they liked playing in royal gardens and catching dragonflies. That and they were expendable political pawns.

God help them all.

A cluttered hallway. A teenage babysitter who stood nervously when they entered the living room, a blue bedroom door—not quite closed. A sleeping child, half buried in bedclothes. These were the images that stayed with him, even as he boarded the plane forty minutes later with both Anastasia and their daughter in tow.

He hadn't been able to stand in that doorway as his daughter awoke, he'd returned to the living room—now minus the babysitter, who had been dismissed. He needed to put some physical distance between them so he could prepare himself for the moment. How to introduce himself to a six-year-old girl who thought her father dead? A child whose life would never be the same now that he'd claimed her as his?

Ana watching him from the doorway to the living room, a child's backpack in hand. He remembered that part.

'There's still time to change your mind,' she'd said. 'You could walk out that door and never look back. You'd never hear from me again. Whatever we had, whatever we once did…it never happened. I will take it to the grave.'

'She's mine.' He'd spread his hands wide. 'She's in

danger because of me. What kind of man would I be—
what kind of father would I be—if I simply stepped back
and let it happen?'

I am not my father.

Therein lay the crux of it.

And here they were on the plane. Ana getting the little one buckled into a seat for take-off. The child sleepy
and wary of everything and everyone, the mother equally
wary, her attention divided wholly between her daughter and him. There was a bedroom on the jet. A supper
room if anyone was hungry. There was comfort here,
and luxury. He didn't know whether to be relieved or
concerned that Ana seemed to have no care whatsoever
for the trappings of royalty or the security team that now
surrounded them.

She'd brought the child to him in the living room of
her house, both her and the girl hastily dressed in clothes
for travelling. Jeans and a soft green pullover for Ana.
Jeans, a teal T-shirt and a soft pink jacket cinched at the
waist for his daughter. Sophia's ponytail had been slightly
lopsided, her amber eyes still bleary with sleep and she
hadn't reminded him of his sister at all in that moment.
She hadn't reminded him of anyone he'd ever met and
that was as it should be.

It had allowed him to breathe.

She was a skinny little thing, this child of his, but she'd
met his gaze fearlessly.

He'd crouched down, one knee to the ground, and held
out his hand for her to shake it. 'Hello.' No way he'd been
able to get his voice to come out smooth so he'd settled for
gruff in the hope that it would hide some of the emotion
welling in his chest at the touch of his daughter's hand.

'Sophia, this is His Royal Highness, Prince Casimir of

Byzenmaach. He's an old acquaintance,' Ana had said. 'And a prince.'

'And your father,' he'd said. Like ripping off a Band-Aid. *Get it done, get it over with.*

The girl had flinched and looked to her mother for confirmation.

'Not dead,' Ana had said somewhat helplessly, and left it at that, and his daughter's wary gaze had returned to his face.

'Your eyes are like mine,' she'd said.

'Yes.'

'Maman says you have a castle,' the girl had said next.

'Yes.' Yes, he did, and he wasn't above using it to impress. 'Would you like to see it?'

'No,' she said.

'And we have puppies,' he'd said.

'What kind of puppies?' She was hard to impress, this daughter of his.

'Wolfhounds.' He'd wondered if a six-year-old would know what that meant. 'They're big and shaggy and built to protect the animals in their care. Wolfhounds are almost as big as ponies, which we also have.'

'Nice try,' Ana had murmured, but, hey. Whatever worked. He wanted his daughter to arrive in Byzenmaach with castles, ponies and puppies on her mind rather than fear in her heart for the unknown.

Ten minutes into the flight he turned on his phone to find three urgent messages waiting, all of them from Rudolpho. 'Flight time is five hours,' he said to Ana as foreboding washed over him. 'There's food, a bed through there with a television screen on the wall. Children's movies.' He'd even stocked up on those. 'Make yourselves comfortable.' He stood and nodded towards the sole woman on his security team. 'Katya will see to your needs.'

Ana eyed Katya with the deep distrust one might afford a rabid dog. 'And what will *you* be doing while we make ourselves at home?' she asked finally.

Casimir wasn't used to having his movements questioned, but for her he made an exception. 'I have some calls I must attend to. There's an office area at the rear of the aircraft.'

'I still have questions,' she said.

'Rest now.' He wished he had that luxury. 'There are some books on Byzenmaach in the bedroom if resting or television doesn't appeal. English editions. Arabic editions.' He'd offer books in his native language now that he knew she could read them. 'You're the mother of a royal bastard and you're about to gain unparalleled access to me and Byzenmaach's most trusted advisors. I want you knowledgeable when it comes to our history, our customs and our politics. I need you to be aware of the political battles in play around you and because of you.'

Not for Anastasia the kind of life his mother had led. Sidelined. Stripped of her voice and unable to influence even the most basic household decisions. Not for Casimir the choices his father had made.

'You expect me to inhale all this knowledge in five hours? From a pile of books?' she said.

'Well, I hear you're very smart and I did choose the books rather carefully,' he offered, deadpan. 'It's a start. I'm arming you with the tools you'll need to navigate my world. Knowledge that will prevent you from becoming a pawn for the ruthless. I *want* you to think for yourself. I *need* you to be able to protect yourself and our daughter. I will never deny you knowledge or a voice.'

She looked at him, and there was something wholly vulnerable in her gaze. A tiny break in her defences against him. 'Is this who you really are? No pretence?'

'This is me.' His world and his choices exposed. Sometimes self-serving, sometimes in service to the crown, sometimes in need of an anchor he didn't have but, heaven help him, he tried to be a fair and just man. And if he could be that for strangers he could sure as hell try to be that for her.

'Okay,' she said quietly.

'Okay,' he echoed, and fled before the sudden sizzling tension in the air between them got too much for him.

CHAPTER THREE

FIVE HOURS AND fifty-eight minutes later, after the flight in the royal jet followed by a helicopter ride, Ana stepped into another world.

Casimir had brought them to a pale stone fortress that shimmered in the moonlight. Floodlights lit the cobblestone courtyard that doubled as the landing pad. The walls of the fortress stretched towards the sky and dark mountains loomed menacingly to either side of it.

Ana couldn't imagine a more remote place.

'They're expecting you,' he said, as a security guard lifted his sleepy daughter from the helicopter and placed her in Ana's arms. 'The south wing is yours for the duration of your stay; they were my mother's rooms and the rooms I used throughout my childhood.' He gestured for a tall, bearded man waiting at the edge of the cobblestones to come forward. 'This is Silas. He'll see to your needs. I'm afraid I have to return to the capital this evening.'

'You're leaving?' If she sounded panicked it was only because she was. He'd stayed in his office for the entire plane flight and had said less than two words to them in the helicopter. Granted, the helicopter was a noisy beast, not conducive to conversation, but still…

'It can't be helped.'

'Why are you leaving? Where are you going?' Ana

clutched Sophia closer. 'Why go to all this trouble to bring us here if you're not even going to *be here*?'

'I'm sorry,' he offered. 'I'll return as soon as I can.'

'You can't just leave us here! I don't even know where here is!'

That'd teach her to take the word of a prince as something worth having.

'You're at the winter fortress in the Belarine Mountains of Byzenmaach. This is my home and the people here are loyal to me. You can trust them.'

'Why on earth would I trust them when I can't even trust *you*?'

He looked torn in that moment. Not to mention utterly weary.

He took her aside, his hand at the small of her back guiding her way, and it was a gesture she'd never forgotten, not to mention a response she'd never experienced with any other man. Desire washed over her, pure and fierce and more potent than ever. Desire laced with fear.

She closed her eyes and drew in a shaky breath. 'I want to trust you to do right by us. I want to believe I've done the right thing by coming here. But I don't know you. I never did. All I know is that you come into my world and turn it upside down and I lose.'

He pressed his lips to her temple and then hesitated before lifting her chin and pressing a kiss to the edge of her lips. His lips were soft and warm and so gentle, and if Ana's eyes fluttered closed and she suddenly wanted this moment to last for ever it was only because all else seemed so harsh.

'I don't want to lose any more,' she whispered, and he pulled away and drew a breath more ragged than hers.

'Neither do I. Believe me, neither do I.' Slowly, almost reluctantly, he tucked a stray strand of hair behind her ear. She leaned into his touch, and maybe it was because he was the one familiar thing in a world that was cold and dark, and maybe her soul would always cry out for his touch no matter what.

'I wanted to help you get settled. I wanted to show you my home, and I will but not tonight. My father is on his deathbed and I've been called to his side. That's what all the phone calls were about—that's where I'm going. And that is no place for a child.' He put his fingers to her chin and tilted her head until she met his gaze. 'We do take care of our young around here, no matter what you might think. Get Silas to show you the puppies. They're real. It's all real.'

'For you,' she said, and he smiled wryly.

'For all of us.'

Ana watched him leave in the helicopter, a fading red light in the bleak night sky, and only once the tail light had disappeared did she realise how cold it was and how heavy six-year-old girls could be. She took a deep breath and felt Sophia's arms tighten around her neck.

'Maman?'

'Hush, baby. Everything's okay. We'll find ourselves another bed soon.'

'Indeed you will,' said the bearded man, bowing slightly. 'Ms Douglas, would you like me to carry the child?'

'No.'

He bowed again. 'Then please let me lead the way to your rooms.'

'Thank you.' She too could be courteous. And it had been one hell of a long evening.

The bedroom suite he took them to was truly fit for a queen. Silk wallpaper adorned the walls. Heavy brocade gold covers graced the bed and Ana wondered whether a body would suffocate beneath the weight of them.

His mother's rooms, he'd said.

The one who'd lost her daughter and committed suicide.

She put Sophia down and fingered the heavy coverlet while the bearded man, Silas, looked on in silence. The floor was a pale grey stone and the ceiling soared high above them. An open fire crackled in the hearth and uniformly shaped logs had been stacked beside it.

There was a breakfast room, a dressing room, a bathroom suite and a nursery, all of it too vast and imposing to contemplate. Tears pricked at her eyes as she stood there, barely holding it together. She closed her eyes, wrapped her arms around her waist and tried to imagine the comfort and familiarity of her snug apartment, but it was no use. She was thousands of miles away and drowning in uncertainty.

Casimir had come for them with conviction in his eyes and promises to protect her on his lips and she'd trusted him to do right by her.

When had he ever done that?

Opening her eyes, she faced her fear as two other people she didn't know brought her and Sophia's luggage into the room and began to open it.

'Leave it,' she snapped.

Her five-minute packing effort; her mess to sort. Their bad luck to be waiting on a woman who didn't want any of this.

The fortress staff withdrew without a word, all except for Silas, who seemed as immovable as the stone beneath her feet. 'We've been warming the suite for two days,' he said. 'I regret that we're not quite ready for visitors but you came as quite a surprise. The chill should be off these rooms by tomorrow and then we can make lighter bedcovers available.'

Castle-warming. Attempting a smile at this point would only bring tears. 'Thank you.'

'What time would you like breakfast?'

'What time is it?' She'd lost track of time, not to mention time zones.

'A little after two a.m., Ms Douglas.'

Right.

'Or you can pick up the phone when you wake, dial one, and let us know when you would like to breakfast.'

She nodded. 'I'd like to ring my parents and let them know where we are. Can I do that from this phone?'

'Of course,' he said. 'Dial zero, then the country code, then the number. It will dial straight out.'

'Thanks.' Not a prisoner then. Not quite. 'I'll do that tonight.' Wake them up. Have a conversation with her parents that she'd been avoiding for almost seven years.

'Of course,' he said again. He turned to Sophia, bowed slightly and left.

Ana waited until the door had closed and they were alone before looking to Sophia. Her daughter's gaze slid towards the nursery room door, her face a study in uncertainty.

'So this is Casimir's castle,' Ana began.

Sophia nodded.

'Big, isn't it?'

Sophia nodded again.

'It'll be better in the morning when we can see it properly. You want to sleep with me tonight?'

A more vigorous nod.

'I can tell you a story before we go to sleep.'

'A story about a princess trapped in a castle and a dragon who comes to save her?' Sophia asked.

'Sure.' They both knew that particular story well. Where were their pyjamas? She hadn't packed winter ones. Why hadn't she packed winter clothes for them?

'Can there be a donkey and a dying king?'

'Yes,' Ana said, still rifling through their suitcases. She knew that story too.

'That man—Cas—he said his father was dying.'

'Yes.'

'And then he *kissed* you.'

Yes. That. Her daughter wasn't used to sharing and Ana had no explanation whatsoever for the kiss. 'Okay, we'll add a dying king and a prince—who is a donkey— to the story.'

'Is he really my father?' Sophia asked abruptly, and there was a world of hurt in her voice and no little accusation.

'Yes.'

'You said he was dead.'

'I know. I thought—' *I thought it better to tell you that than the truth.* 'I thought wrong.'

'What does he want?' Sophia asked next.

'Right now he wants to protect us.' Give the devil his due. 'And then I think he wants to get to know you.'

'You're not leaving me here and going home, are you?' Fierce golden eyes were even more breathtaking when they were vulnerable.

'No. I will never do that.'

'Promise?'

'I promise. What else do you want in this story?'

'No frogs.'

'Got it. No frogs.'

'And no kisses,' Sophia said fiercely.

'Not even a mother's goodnight kiss for the princess?'

Sophia hesitated. 'Am I a princess?'

Pyjamas! Finally. 'Here. Get changed and jump into bed and then there will be storytelling. As for whether you're a princess or not... I don't know. Your father's a prince. He's about to become a king. But he and I aren't married, and that complicates things. It's something else to ask when we see him next.'

Mothers were wise, and it was their duty to make chewable that which was complex. Or, in this case, to avoid talking about Casimir altogether.

'So. Let me tell you a story about a castle and a dragon and a princess. You want to hear it in Russian or in French?'

An hour later, Sophia was asleep and Ana was in the other room, castle phone in hand and too afraid to use it. She needed advice and with that came confession. For seven years she'd shut her parents out as far as the identity of Sophia's father was concerned. They'd helped her get back on her feet after Sophia had been born. With their financial help she'd been able to continue her studies and find childcare for her baby. They hadn't let her fall. They'd supported her.

But they'd never, ever understood her choices.

She barely understood them herself.

She made the call and started pacing the moment she heard her mother's voice.

'I don't want you to worry,' she said to begin with, and knew it for an opening that would guarantee exactly the opposite result.

'I'm in Byzenmaach with Sophia...and Sophia's father,' she said next, and, yeah, she truly failed at giving reassurances. 'Let me start again.'

'Anastasia, breathe,' her mother said, so she did.

'Now, start from the beginning.'

'Oh, you really don't want me to do that.'

'I really do,' her mother said gently. 'If this is about Sophia's father, I really do want you to start from the beginning.'

She couldn't do it.

'Let me start for you,' her mother said next. Still calm. No judgement. 'You were nineteen and I'd just sent you away from me for the very first time. A new country for you. A bright future. I knew you were precocious, passionate, full of life and I wanted new experiences for you. New people to meet and worlds to explore. I thought I'd prepared you.'

'You did. Mama, you did. None of this was your fault.'

'And then you met a man.'

'He was twenty-three, and he was everything.' Ana gave her that in the hope that her next words would come more easily. 'He said his name was Cas and that he'd been attending a political summit in Geneva. He stayed with me for a week. It was a good week. A week out of time and place—I was so captivated by him. And then he left. You know he left.' She closed her eyes. 'I found out who he was just before Sophia was born, and then it made sense. What he'd done. Why he went away and never looked back. He's the Crown Prince of Byzenmaach. Sole heir to the throne and he's promised elsewhere. His father is dying and he'll be king within days. I didn't know that to start with, but I've known for a while.'

Silence held sway while her mother digested her words. Her mother was a political animal, first and foremost. Ana didn't need to say any more.

'And now he wants Sophia,' her mother offered at last.

'Yes.'

'Oh, baby,' her mother said, and there was no solution in those words, just a deep well of compassion and unshed tears.

'So I'm here, in Byzenmaach, trying to find a way forward that doesn't involve giving her up or me turning into some kind of royal wallpaper without any agency or life of my own.' That was the sum of it. The end result of all those decisions made long ago. 'I'm sorry I never told you who he was. I never thought he'd return. I thought it better that no one knew. Safer for everyone.'

'Oh, Ana.'

'Don't make me cry,' Ana said fiercely. 'I can't cry here. I can't show weakness. They'll know I'm not enough. That I've never been enough.'

'You have *always* been enough.' Her mother had slipped into Russian, a sure sign of emotions fully engaged. 'I am so proud of you. I have always been proud of you. And if he left you because he couldn't see your value, that's *his* loss. And your advantage.'

'Mama, what do I do? Can I fight a royal family for Sophia and win?'

Her mother's silence echoed what she already knew.

'What do I do?'

Her mother drew a deep breath. 'So he's about to marry?'

'I don't know. I think so.'

'What are your feelings for him?'

'I don't know.'

'Oh,' her mother said.

'What do you mean, "*Oh*"?'

'I mean he's it for you, and always has been.'

'No!'

Maybe.

'Okay, maybe feelings are involved and I'm not as immune to him as I'd like to be. He's…more than he used to be. More of everything.'

'This is bad,' her mother said. 'Anastasia, listen to me. You keep your feelings for him to yourself for now. It's to his advantage that you still care for him, not yours. Negotiate first. Confess your attraction later. Or never. Never would work.'

'Got it.' Ana stifled a snort.

'Anastasia, your experience with men is—'

'Limited. I know. But when you've had the best why settle for less?'

'He wasn't the best. He left you. Remember that? Because I do.'

'I remember.'

'You never gave anyone else even half a chance. You threw yourself into your work, and that worked for you and continues to do so. But don't try and tell me you live for your career. Because I live for mine, and God bless your father for putting up with me in that regard, but you're not like me. You don't have that compulsion. You work because that was the plan before he came into your life and you were determined to stick to the plan afterwards. And you have. And I'm proud of all that you've achieved. But your work is not your life's ambition. It's just ambition.'

'Mama, I don't—'

'You want the fairy tale, Anastasia. An identity of your own, the man you love at your side and children in your life and in your heart. Sophia and more. That's your life's ambition. Correct me if I'm wrong.'

Ana nudged her forehead gently against the wall, phone at her ear and bare feet on cold stone. 'You're not wrong.'

'It's not too much to ask for. This I believe. Will he give that to you?'

'No.'

'Negotiate,' said her mother, and this time Ana laughed helplessly.

'With what?'

'Yourself.'

'You mean the one he left all those years ago? Couldn't hold his attention for more than a week?'

'His mistake. He didn't realise what he held.'

'Maybe he did.'

'*Or* you can take a good look at him without the rose-coloured glasses of youth and this time you look for the flaws in him.' Her mother's voice had firmed. 'Embrace him or not, but see him for who he is and bargain hard for your future and Sophia's. I raised a daughter with brains as well as heart. Don't prove me wrong.'

'So find his weakness and exploit it?'

'Well, that's another way of putting it,' her mother said drily. 'That or make him see you and want you and love you the way you should be loved.'

'How is that easy to do?'

'It can be.' Her mother sighed. 'If he's the right one for you, it's as easy as breathing.'

'I'm not breathing, Mama. I'm holding my breath.' She looked around the room, at the ceilings high above her with their intricate plasterwork, at the silk wallpaper and the paintings on the walls. 'I don't know how to do this.'

'You're not alone. Remember that. There's strength in that. You have us, and Sophia. You *know* love and that is the strongest force in the world. Does he know love?'

Ana thought of the man and his history. His duty and his resolve. 'I don't know.'

'Step one,' said her mother. 'Find out.'

CHAPTER FOUR

CASIMIR'S FATHER DIED sixteen hours after Casimir reached the royal palace. Casimir had sat at his father's bedside and occasionally held the older man's hand and tried to feel something other than bone-deep weariness. His father had rallied at one point, enough to realise that Cas was there, but beyond that there had been no real communication.

Cas would never know what words his father spoke at the very end; they'd been unintelligible. He didn't need to know. His father had never spoken any words of love in Casimir's presence and Casimir would have been astonished to hear any, even here at the end of things.

When his father took his last breath, Cas felt nothing. No sorrow. No grief. He knew grief and this wasn't it. He just felt blank.

He waited five minutes before calling the physicians in. Five minutes that he spent with his head bowed and his hand still clasped in his father's until finally he felt a small stirring of some kind of feeling, even if it was only relief for the end of his father's suffering.

His father was at rest now. No more brutal physical pain for the man who'd once been king. This was a good thing.

When he opened the huge double doors of his father's

bedchamber and stepped out into the anteroom, every man and woman waiting stood and snapped to attention.

'It's finished,' he told them. 'The king is dead.'

Rudolpho was the first to respond. 'Long live the king.'

And there it was. Another king for the Byzenmaach throne.

His father's endgame finally realised.

Casimir rubbed at his face, beyond tired and way beyond lucid. Sixteen hours at his father's bedside. Twelve hours of travel before that, with collecting Ana and Sophia somewhere in the middle of it. A full day's work before he'd even left to go and get them. Thirty-six hours since he'd last slept and still more to do before he could rest. 'I'm going home,' he said.

'Your Majesty.' Rudolpho again, eyeing him as cautiously as one might survey a ticking time bomb. 'There are rooms here. Surely—'

'I'm going home,' he said again. He'd stood vigil to the bitter end and no one could fault him. Duty had been served and all he wanted was to get out of this place and breathe for a while before he had to return.

Ana was waiting for him. That, more than anything, drew him like a lodestone. 'Make it happen.'

'Yes, Your Majesty.' Rudolpho bowed and Casimir almost groaned. He'd spent a lifetime preparing for this moment, and here he was acting like a petty two-year-old. 'I also want every portrait and photo of my sister and mother gone from these palace walls by the time I return. All bar the two in the portrait gallery. They can stay.'

Someone gasped. This wasn't going well. That second command could have waited a decade or so before being made. Casimir had waited all of seven minutes. He smiled grimly and tried to explain himself—another first in a day of firsts. 'Put them in a room somewhere and shut the door on them. My family will never be forgotten—not by me, not by any of you. This I know. But this palace has served as a shrine to the dead long enough. No more. Not one minute more.'

People bowed their heads. His father's people, not wanting to make eye contact.

His people now.

He'd carried the hope of a nation on his shoulders for years and it was finally time to deliver.

'I will serve,' he rasped. 'To the best of my ability I will serve you all. When have I not? But I am *not* my father, and things *will* change around here. Not in five years' time, not in ten. Change starts now.'

It wasn't until he and Rudolpho were approaching the helicopter ten minutes later that the old advisor deigned to talk about Casimir's first words in his new role.

'Good pep talk,' Rudolpho offered drily. 'You could have warned me about wanting to take the portraits down.'

Could've. Didn't. 'I wanted to see their reactions for myself.'

'And what did their reactions tell you?'

'That some will always resist change and others will embrace it.'

'You didn't need to issue a royal command to know that.'

Casimir smiled mirthlessly. 'I also learned that the people of Byzenmaach are willing to give me more leeway than I expected, going forward. And I'm going to take it.'

'You'll be needing a new chief advisor, I presume,' Rudolpho offered tightly.

'No. I want you to stay on in the role, but there's a

catch. I don't want the kind of silent subservience you gave my father. I know how you work. You sidle in sideways, using your considerable diplomacy skills to smooth over problems that you knew my father would never outright address. That stops. For forty years you've had the pulse of a nation at your fingertips. Now you have a voice to go with it and I expect you to use it, because I'm listening. I'd like to see if together we *can* fix what my father would not. Are you up for it?'

'Your Majesty, I am most definitely *up for it*, as it were. Although not entirely fluent in your vernacular.'

'That's all right.' Casimir allowed himself a smile. 'You'll learn.'

The first thing Casimir saw as he approached the winter fortress by air were the flags flying at half-mast. So they knew and there would be no need to say it again. The king was dead. Byzenmaach was his now, not that it mattered here in the cradle of these mountains.

The people here had always been his.

By the time they'd landed and he'd reached the entrance hall, it seemed as if the entire castle staff had either seen or heard the helicopter land and dropped whatever they were doing.

People lined up to one side of the door. People who'd cared for him since he was a child. People he cared for, like Silas and his wife, Lor. People like Tomas the falconer and Saul the stable master.

God help him, he was tired.

But he did what he had to do. He started at the top of the line and took an old groundsman's hand in his and let the man offer his condolences. He would speak to his people until there was no one left in line that he hadn't touched and listened to. He would do this because, unlike his father's courtiers, he owed them.

He looked away from the person in front of him just once—looked up to see how far the line stretched—and there stood Ana at the foot of the stairs, with Sophia beside her. He smiled, and maybe it was a mere echo of the smiles they'd shared all those years ago, but it was real.

She looked well rested and coolly composed. Guarded, which wasn't surprising. He'd all but abandoned her here. She lifted her chin and stared him down as if she belonged here and he had some explaining to do, dead father or not.

Ten more minutes and he'd be at the end of the line and facing her and the daughter he'd barely come to terms with.

If this was protocol, Ana didn't know her part in it, other than to hover by the foot of the stairs with Sophia at her side and wait for Casimir to approach them.

Casimir's father was dead. Byzenmaach had a new king and he was it, as evidenced by the security staff who accompanied him. Hard-eyed men and women in dark suits, they took up positions in corridors, by doorways and on the stairs.

Not alarming at all.

Cas made a point of greeting every person waiting to speak with him. He shook every hand and accepted a lone poppy from a wizened woman who couldn't possibly still work for him. He patted the woman's hand and whispered something that made her smile, and then he reached Silas and his wife, Lor, and Ana was surprised at the strength of the embrace they shared. Words passed in that embrace, none of them spoken. Whispers of the boy he'd once been and exactly where such a boy might have found a comforting hand.

And then he turned his gaze on her and Sophia and the conflict in his eyes rendered her silent.

She was here at his request, sure enough, but she had no idea if he wanted her and Sophia where he could see them.

He smiled at her then, a touch of wry amusement in the curve of it, and in that instant became the man she'd once known.

'My condolences,' she said, so stilted and formal, but she didn't know what else to say.

'Thank you,' he said quietly. 'Ana. Sophia. Once again I must apologise for leaving you to your own devices. It appears my skills as a host are gravely overrated.'

'We have puppies,' Sophia said by way of reply, and it was the right thing to say. Or perhaps it simply wasn't the wrong thing to say.

'*Do* we?' he said.

'Do you want to see them?' her daughter asked.

'Yes.'

'They're Jelly's,' Sophia added. 'They're very special. Lor says you named Jelly the First when you were a kid.'

'I did,' he said.

'This mother dog is Jelly the Eighth. Which means one of the puppies has to be called Jelly the Ninth.'

'Have you chosen which one yet?' he asked.

'Yes.' Sophia rushed ahead and then stopped abruptly at the first security guard, glancing back at Cas to see if he was following and then at Ana. Or perhaps she was simply looking for permission to proceed.

Ana stood frozen, not knowing her role in any of this. And then Casimir turned to her and pinned her with a questioning gaze as well. 'Coming?' he asked.

Yes. Even with the way she usually drew public gaze, she was hard pressed not to flinch beneath the weight of *this* crowd's gaze. Wariness. Suspicion. Not from Silas or Lor, who she'd spent most of the day with, but from others, yes. She could feel the crawl of judgement on her skin.

It made her straighten her shoulders and lift her chin as she walked towards him. 'Thank you for coming back here this evening,' she said when she reached him.

'Did you think I wouldn't?'

'I didn't know. I know nothing of the duties of a king.'

They reached the kitchen, not that it was like any other kitchen Ana had ever been in. This kitchen had store-rooms of its own and a long central bench. Three hearths, only one of which was functional. One of the other fireplaces held Jelly the wolfhound and her puppies. Sophia approached them with a confidence borne of innocence, dropping first to her knees and then to her belly, her ponytail off-centre again and her too-short jeans hiking halfway up her calves. She wasn't wearing shoes. Who wore shoes inside a house?

Unless, of course, the house was a royal fortress.

'This one's Little Jelly,' Sophia said, gently stroking one of the puppies while Mama Jelly looked on indulgently.

Wolfhounds were placid and tolerant, Ana had decided. This one was, at any rate.

'How can you tell?' Casimir asked.

'She has a white tip on her tail, just like Big Jelly.'

'I think Sophia's going to be a geneticist,' Ana murmured, given all the questions she'd asked about eye colours today. 'Have you eaten?' Not that it was her place to ask, but it was as good a question as any. A regular question without any ulterior weight to it. 'Lor's been baking all day.'

'I'm not hungry,' he said, but he went into a side chamber and returned shortly after with a bottle of whisky. He knew where the tumblers were and enquired, with the tilt of the bottle, whether he should fill a glass for her.

'No,' she said.

'Something else?' he asked as he poured himself one.

'I'm fine.'

'What have you been doing today?' he asked next.

'That's really what you want to talk about?'

'Yes.' A weary smile crossed his lips and softened her heart. He looked to their daughter, the wolfhound and the puppies. 'Talk to me of carefree things.'

'We baked with Lor and made Turkish delight.'

'My favourite,' he said.

'So Lor said.' Ana knew a lot of things about him that she hadn't known before this morning, including the fact that dead King Leonidas had been a good king, a merciless opponent, an indifferent husband and a hard father to please. 'Then we saw falcons and horses and hand fed them both. Then there's the bathhouse,' she added, and was rewarded with the glimmer of a smile.

'You found it?'

'Oh, I did,' she said reverently.

'You liked it?'

It was a Roman gladiator's bathhouse built of marble, with steaming hot pools of varying temperature and a waterfall. A soaring domed roof added majesty. 'I want to take it with me when I leave.'

'You're not the first to want that.' His gaze drifted to Sophia again. 'I know we need to talk about what I have in mind for you both. I should be free of my most pressing commitments by Wednesday at the latest.'

It was Saturday night.

'Cas.' As beautiful as this place was, she couldn't just abandon the life she'd built on the off-chance that the new king of Byzenmaach could schedule her in. 'I need to understand what you want from us now, not next week. I need you to prioritise our custody talks. Can you do that for me? Because I guarantee that if you can't do that I'm going to assume that you will *never* put your daughter's needs first.'

He met her gaze squarely. 'Tell me what you want going forward.'

'Ideally? The security threat you spoke of gone, full custody of my daughter, and my life in Geneva to resume.'

He nodded. 'I'm working on the first, no to the second, no idea about the third. Like it or not, your daughter is a part of the royal family of Byzenmaach now and, by extension, so are you. Complications will ensue.'

'I want to meet with you tomorrow to talk about a way forward for us all,' she continued doggedly, keeping her mother's words of negotiation firmly in mind. 'I want to talk about the kind of compromises we may *both* need to make. No lawyers. Not yet. Just you, me, a problem to solve and our goodwill.'

'I have meetings all morning.'

'Or…you can toss my current goodwill back in my face and we can embark on a very public, very bitter custody battle. Then we can get *all* the lawyers involved,' she murmured. 'UK lawyers. Human rights lawyers. *Your* lawyers. Keep in mind that when it comes to eviscerating reputations I have a great deal less to lose than you.'

Those fierce tawny eyes of his narrowed. 'Where'd you learn to negotiate?'

'The UN.'

He smiled mirthlessly and lifted the glass to his lips for another hit. 'Right.'

'I'm not nineteen and naïve any more, Casimir. I can't

afford to be. And you're not twenty-three and running from your responsibilities. Or are you still doing that?'

'Ana, leave off. You've got your meeting tomorrow. I'll make time.'

'Thank you.' It didn't feel like victory. Instead, it felt a whole lot like kicking a man when he was down. She sipped at her drink as he studied his daughter and the puppies as if they were puzzle pieces he couldn't quite place. And this time when he spoke he didn't look at her.

'My father used to say to me, "You need to marry and produce an heir, Casimir, for the sake of the throne". I used to tell him there was plenty of time for that, and when I turned thirty I would do my duty by him and by Byzenmaach. Until then, I didn't *want* to be bound within marriage. I didn't want to bring children into my world. Because I knew I'd fear for their safety in a way that I've never feared for my own.' He ducked his head and ran a hand through his hair before turning his gaze on them again. 'For what it's worth, I was right. Some of my fears for your safety and for hers aren't even based in reality. They're just shadows. Intangible. Present only in my head, and I don't know how to get rid of them.'

'Maybe I can help,' she offered quietly.

The look he gave her in return was a shadowy, twisted thing.

'Even if it's simply to cut you some slack when it comes to intangible fears based on some of your more formative experiences,' she said. 'In return, you might cut me some slack when it comes to my fear of losing Sophia to a glittering, privileged world I cannot access.'

'Done,' he muttered. 'I am no monster to deny a mother access to her child. We'll work something out.'

'What are you going to do about a legitimate heir?' It

wasn't an idle question. Clearly, he needed an heir. That was his reality. 'I'm assuming Sophia will never inherit?'

'Correct. Sophia will never rule Byzenmaach. It doesn't make her any less valuable in my eyes. She's my daughter and I am more than glad she exists, and I am…grateful…' he chose the word as if trying it on for size '… I am grateful you are here with me today. Both of you. Like this.'

'You have no other family left.' She tried to imagine herself all alone in the world, and couldn't. She too would cling to whatever slim thread presented itself. 'Better this than nothing.'

'That's not it.' Her gaze met his and held and he was the first to look away. 'Hell, maybe it is.' He took a drink. 'Do you ever think about back then? About what we had?'

'Yes.' Pointless denying it.

'Good thoughts?'

'Sometimes,' she offered. 'We were very good at some things. Sleep wasn't one of them.' She watched his lips tilt slightly and knew she wanted more of that and less of the duty-bound monarch who'd entered his fortress and set to making sure his people were comforted.

'There wasn't much cooking happening either,' he rasped.

'You couldn't cook. That was blindingly obvious.' She looked around the huge catering kitchen that was Lor's domain, for all that the older woman was staying out of it at present. 'And now I know why.'

'Never saw the need to learn,' he admitted. 'Do you still live on apple Danishes and sunshine?'

'Sometimes I try.' Not often. Too many sweets and her curves tended to get out of control. She wondered if he'd clocked the changes in her figure in the same way she'd noticed the increased breadth of his shoulders and the muscles in his thighs. She wondered if he was looking for traces of the laughing girl she'd once been in the same way she was waiting for him to be the person she remembered. The one with the smile she'd never had to work for. The one whose body had been hers for the taking.

He'd had her every which way and then some.

She hadn't forgotten.

'Yeah. It's not hard to look back on that week with a certain amount of fondness.' Even his wrists, currently half covered by the snowy white cuffs of his shirt, conjured memories of their lovemaking. Of her pinning his arms above his head the better to get at him, and of him letting her. 'And then you left.'

He said nothing.

Nothing to explain.

'So. Do you have any other illegitimate offspring I should know about?' she asked.

'No.'

'Are you sure? I mean, you didn't know about Sophia until now. Maybe there's more.'

'There's not.'

'How do you know?' She was goading him now, for no real purpose other than she wanted to hurt him the way he was hurting her.

'Because I've never been as careless as I was with you, neither before nor since. Nor have I ever deceived another the way I did you.'

And wasn't that adding fuel to an already lit flame. 'Then why did you do it? *To me!* What did I ever do to you to deserve that kind of treatment except love you? *I don't understand.*' She'd never understood.

'I saw something I wanted and took it. I never thought beyond the moment as to whether I could keep it. Never a good idea.' He stood abruptly and drained his glass.

'But it's done now, and it's time to move forward. Perhaps after you put Sophia to bed you can come and find me. We can try more negotiation, maybe even work our way up to argument.'

'Will you even be awake? When did you last sleep?' And why did she care?

'Centuries ago,' he offered. 'You have the advantage. Take it or leave it.'

'I'll take it,' she said.

Casimir knew he was making a mess of things when it came to his dealings with Ana. Incorporating her and Sophia into his life was never going to be easy—and this was only the beginning. They'd had only the tiniest taste of the security needed to keep them safe, and no encounters whatsoever with the press. Even if he had been willing to let his daughter live in Geneva some of the time—and he wasn't—fundamental changes would have to be made to the way they lived.

Casimir's bedroom provided the solitude he so badly needed. Cold meats, cheeses and breads had been laid out on the sideboard. Lor's doing, most likely, for she well knew his tendency to skip meals when at the palace.

Shower first, eat later. He needed the smell of death gone, never mind that all he had to do was close his eyes in order to conjure a vision of it.

He stripped as he walked towards the bathroom. Stood naked under the stinging spray and finally let the significance of this day enter the guarded chambers of his heart. His father was dead and he still couldn't summon true grief for him. He tried to think back, and further back again, but couldn't call up a memory of his father ever letting his royal façade fall. It wasn't done. Duty to the throne had been everything.

Casimir *knew* what his father would do with Sophia in this situation. Use her as a panacea for the nation and milk her resemblance to Claudia for all it was worth until a *real* heir could be produced. What would his father have done with her after that? Shipped her back into obscurity? Married her off in service to Byzenmaach alliances? Either way, his father would never have allowed a daughter close enough to be missed.

His father would certainly never have allowed any wife or mother of that child—or even the child herself—any say in those decisions.

I am not him.

That sentiment right there was his weakness when it came to dealing with Ana and Sophia. Was he to be so bound up in proving himself a more reasonable man than his father that he forgot to voice what *he* wanted out of this? To raise a daughter who had no doubt whatsoever as to her father's love for her. That was a primary goal of his.

And there it was again, that insidious comparison to his upbringing. His father's influence worming its way into every breath.

His father was dead.

And if Casimir felt only a bone-deep relief, so be it.

It wasn't the hard-hearted indifference his father had tried to instil in him and for that he would be grateful. His father was dead and he had a daughter who lived and breathed and he wanted nothing more than to have her within reach so he could get to know her. He didn't want to parent her alone. He didn't want to cut Ana out of her life.

He wanted them both within reach, and when it came to Ana…

When it came to her he'd always wanted more than he could afford.

Why was it that the mere thought of Anastasia Douglas could make even the most exhausted version of himself rise to the occasion?

New memories to replace the old, and now he had one of her waiting for him on the stairs to his fortress and smiling when he looked her way. He had one of her pouring him a drink, all understated care and compassion. Her smile when she'd told him she'd already discovered the sensory pleasures of the bathhouse. He'd not forget that any time soon.

Still too open and honest for her own good, this new Ana.

Still way too inclined to look at him and let her gaze linger on his fingers and his mouth, his body and the rise and fall of his chest. It was still there, that overwhelming awareness of each other. He still wanted her with every breath he took.

And she wasn't indifferent to him.

It was going to make negotiating a pathway forward more difficult for all of them.

What else did he want from her? That was the question. Forget the demands of the monarchy for once. Forget his father's example when it came to dealing with women.

What *else* did he want from her if he could have it?

Apart from her—wholly naked and pleading—beneath him.

Five minutes later he emerged from the shower, his skin still dripping and his towel slung low around his hips. He felt a little more human, a little more alert, and no more the wiser.

Ana stood waiting for him.

'Silas told me where to find you,' she said.

'Did he tell you to walk right on into my private quarters?'

'You invited me.'

So he had. The why of it still escaped him. He was too tired for negotiation and at a disadvantage. If she pressed him for concessions he was likely to give them. Was it loneliness that had made him extend the invitation? Did he have any idea why he was doing this?

All food for thought.

'This room is the mirror of the one I'm in. Only warmer.' Her gaze never left his skin. 'I was looking at it before you came in. Shouldn't you be putting some clothes on?'

'Perhaps if I'd known you were here...' Although, given the hot colour stealing through her cheeks, he might have left them off just for her. 'Nothing you haven't seen before.'

'You look like an Egyptian king.'

'Well, you know. Romans, Egyptians. Relatives. All of them.' She couldn't seem to drag her gaze away from him and he knew that if she kept it up he'd be reaching for her within minutes. 'Do you feel like swimming? I feel like swimming.' He walked towards the door that led to the walkway that led to the bathhouse. She'd know where he was heading soon enough given that her rooms had the mirror image layout and bathhouse access. 'You don't look as angry with me as you did in the kitchen.'

'I'm trying to be a grown-up. Also, you've had a hard few days. I'll give you that.'

'Always with the compliments,' he said. Broken moonlight banded the stone floor and faintly lit the way. 'Coming?'

'You say that a lot.'

'King,' he said. 'People wait on my command.'

'Even your lovers? Even your friends? When does equal exchange happen?'

Rarely, and maybe that was part of his problem. 'Perhaps you can show me how it's done.'

She fell into step beside him, their shoulders brushing every so often, never mind that the walkway was comfortably wide enough for two.

'How's this going to work?' she murmured. 'You swim, I talk and if you don't like what I have to say you disappear underwater?'

'Well, it *could* work that way,' he murmured agreeably. 'Or you could swim too.'

'No costume.'

'Are you expecting me to wear one?' Now there was a thought he hadn't entertained.

'Sophia wants to know if she's a princess,' Ana said next. 'My mother also wants to know about Sophia's princess status. I don't know what to tell them.'

'Officially, no. Unofficially, yes.'

'Good luck explaining that to a six-year-old.'

'My sister's duchy lies vacant. I find it fitting that it goes to Sophia, in which case she'll hold the title of duchess. There is a castle to go with it. A very pretty one. Will that suffice?'

The walkway chilled his skin. Talk of tiny princesses did likewise. Ana's presence heated it. All in all, there was balance.

'Are you really serious about making Sophia a part of the royal family?' she asked.

'Did you think I wouldn't be?'

'I thought you were offering us protection on an as-needed basis. Not…incorporation.'

'I'm offering both. She's my daughter too, Anastasia. My blood. I have a duty of care. Had I known of her existence—'

But he hadn't known. He'd never, ever thought there'd

be those kind of consequences. Ana had been so determined to have a career.

'I should have known about her. Followed up with you. I should have made it my business to know.' He was not flawless. He could admit that. 'Now that I do know I will not do wrong by you. Sophia will need a nanny while she's here. Tutors,' he continued, and his daughter wasn't the only one who'd need tutoring. 'Would you object to me providing a tutor for you? I would have you educated in royal protocol and diplomacy so that you in turn can guide our daughter. I meant what I said about not cutting you out of Sophia's life. That's not what I want.'

She was silent a long time after that, and he wondered if he'd offended her. He hadn't, had he? He'd offered a service. Politely.

They reached the bathing room and stepped inside, and he'd switched on the underwater lights before she finally answered.

'I don't object to being tutored,' she murmured. 'I would like to be involved in helping Sophia make the transition from ordinary girl to... Duchess.'

'I'll make it happen,' he said. He padded towards his favourite pool. It was smaller than the others, hotter, and set back into the shadows. No underwater lights for this pool. It was all dark, lapping water and unspoken promise.

'Have you made any progress when it comes to knowing why we were under surveillance in Geneva?' she asked.

'Not yet.'

'What happens when the two weeks is up and your people still don't know what they want?'

'You stay here.' Where he wanted her.

'If safety is to be an ongoing issue for Sophia, why

not simply put protection measures in place for us in Geneva?'

Because they wouldn't be enough for his peace of mind. 'I want to make you an offer,' he told her instead. 'I want you and Sophia to live in Byzenmaach on a permanent basis. In return I will do everything in my power to ensure your career as an interpreter continues.'

'In Byzenmaach,' she said flatly, her eyes shadowed.

'That's right. I can offer you ongoing comfort and security in any number of living situations. Not necessarily here. You could have more independence than this. You could create new career opportunities and the palace would help with that. I truly don't regard the offer as a bad one.'

'*This* is your idea of negotiating a way forward for us all?'

Yes. 'And now you speak and tell me what you do and don't like about the offer. And I listen and take it into account.' He dropped his towel and walked to the side of the pool.

'Are you deliberately trying to distract me with your naked self?' There was frustration in her voice, liberally mixed with something that sounded like want.

'All's fair in love and negotiation. Is it working?'

'Well, you're even more spectacular naked than I remembered, so I'm going to have to go with yes.'

'Are you coming in? It's very pleasant.'

'I know it's very pleasant,' she muttered grudgingly, but she made no move to undress. 'I want Sophia to live with me in Geneva. She can visit you at weekends.'

'No.'

'I want to keep working for the UN.'

'A travel account will be set up so you can move freely between countries and residences. You'll have more freedom to pick and choose the work you undertake than you ever had before as a single mother. You're good at what you do, Anastasia. I have every confidence you can turn my offer into a career-enhancing move, assuming career progress is truly what you're interested in.'

She scowled at him and said nothing.

'It will, of course, be necessary to inform the palace of your plans from now on, whether you're in possession of Sophia or not. You'll have access to my secretary.'

'And do I get to know *your* every move from now on?' she enquired a little too dulcetly for comfort.

'You will know where Sophia is at all times.' His daughter was going to need a secretary of her own at this rate. 'She will, of course, have a security detail on her, no matter where she is. She's a target now.'

'And you'd like me to thank you for making her one?'

It didn't seem likely that she was going to thank him for any of it. Casimir let the hot spring water soothe his body and quiet his mind. 'I'm currently undecided as to the type of security you will require on an ongoing basis,' he told her.

Ana had stopped to toe off her shoes. The noise the zip of her skirt made carried across the water with a sibilant hiss and gave him a moment's warning before the dark material pooled at her feet. Her legs glowed porcelain pale and her underwear was tiny and white. Casimir swallowed hard.

Whose idea had it been to get naked and swim? Because the stirring in his body declared it a bad one.

He cleared his throat. 'Are we still negotiating?'

'Is that what you call this?'

Her top had joined her skirt on the floor. Her bra was nothing but lace and shoestrings but at least she kept it on as she knelt at the side of the pool and trailed her fingers in the water. 'I am not a puppet to be made to dance on your strings. I have opinions. A life to lead.'

'I'm listening.'

'Casimir, whatever it is you think you're doing…listening's not it.'

She had more curves than she'd had at nineteen. His body thought it'd be a fine idea to reacquaint himself with them, map them with hands and lips, see how they fitted.

'Hell with it,' he murmured. 'The press will never leave you alone once they get a good look at you. You're getting a full security detail as well. And a press liaison. They're going to eat you alive.'

'There you go again. Telling me what's going to happen.'

'Or you could go without the press liaison and beg me for one later, once the damage has been done. Trust me; if you want to have control over any of this, you need to control your own spin. I'm giving you the means to do that.'

'Uh huh.' She slipped into the pool with barely a splash, the water licking at her skin and raising goosebumps, never mind its warmth. Her eyes were dark and troubled when they landed on him.

'If—once you've become more accustomed to your role within the royal scheme of things—you find this to be overkill, let me know and I'll back it off a little,' he offered.

'You really do think you're negotiating.' She sounded more amazed than grateful. 'What if I don't *want* to live in Byzenmaach and be connected to the throne?'

'It's not all bad, Ana. Money and comfort will never be a concern for you again.'

'They never *have* been a concern of mine. I live comfortably enough already.'

'You will have influence.'

'Over who? Over you?'

'When it comes to our daughter you will always have my ear,' he told her.

'What good is that? Your ears don't work. All you do is talk.' Her eyes skittered to his lips. When she raised her gaze to him again, those all-seeing eyes were knowing and somewhat resigned.

'You bore a royal child, Anastasia. Surely you knew that some day it would come to this.'

'No, Cas. I bore *your* child. The child of the man I met seven years ago. The one who made me feel loved and cherished and brought me hot croissants from the bakery every morning. The one with the sweet tooth and the wicked tongue. We were careful—you were there. Pregnancy wasn't part of your plan or mine. And still it happened and you were already long gone. I bore a love child, not a royal one.'

He'd lied to her. There was no getting past that. He had no excuse for his deceit other than he'd met her and fallen utterly in thrall. One week, just one, in which royal duty hadn't ruled him.

'I'm resentful.' She drew closer. 'Damn right I am. Last time you came into my life you changed the shape of it completely. You're doing it again.'

Tension. So much tension between them and only part of it due to argument. Still so strong this invisible thing between them. 'Maybe I want to leave your life in better shape than I left it in last time,' he said.

'Maybe you just want what you can't have.'

Maybe he did. She didn't back away when he bent his lips to hers. He kissed her gently, at first. A hello that devolved into piercing heat within moments. She tasted of sweetness and surrender, succour and temptation, and the need in him was so big. Seven years since he'd lost himself to this and he needed it again with a ferocity he couldn't quite handle.

This night, with his father dead and not yet buried and the weight of the crown heavy on his head. This place that had always been a haven to him. This woman, whose passionate surrender had never failed to rouse him. Peel away the layers until she breathed only for him, Casimir the man and not Casimir the king.

The kiss deepened as he splayed his hands around her waist and drew her in. One hand to the small of her back now, as his erection met supple skin.

'You still want me,' she murmured.

'And you want me.' He dipped his head to her neck, to the swell of her breast and then to its peak and proved his point.

She proved it again when she scored her nails across his neck and kept him there.

'Just so you know,' she murmured raggedly. 'If you take me now and marry another, I will make your life a living hell.'

'I'm used to it,' he muttered, and claimed her mouth again.

She didn't fight him. Not when he took her to the steps leading down into the pool and laid her out on them before they both drowned. Not when he worshipped her with kisses and covetous hands. His hand to her ankle as he raised her knee to her breast. A kiss for the hollow behind the knee. The roughness of his cheek and chin against the flawless skin of her inner thigh. Delicacy after that, as he set his mouth to her. No need for a map; he already knew how to read every twitch she made and memory did not fail him.

She came on his tongue with a cry and a shudder that

started deep within and rippled out, and nothing else mattered but conquering her all over again, with him inside her this time. He'd never been bare inside her before and he wanted to feel it.

It would be madness to risk it.

'Whose idea was it to trade my bed for marble?' he muttered as he eased her away and helped her to her feet.

'Yours.'

'Bathing *after* sex. Remind me next time.' And then he was dragging her through the door and out onto the walkway. He'd taken all of two strides before another fantasy took hold. Him. Her. Stone walls and a valley far below them as he slaked his need for her beneath the moonlight.

He didn't think they were going to make it to the bed.

He pushed her up against a stone column, his fingers laced in hers and hers above her head. She uttered a broken curse and sank into his kiss as if born for it.

'I never forgot,' he whispered, knowing it for confession. A power exchange he could never deny, no matter what happened going forward.

'I wept when you left,' she said between kisses.

One hand was to her wrists now, his other around the curve of her buttock to urge her closer, her leg outside his—he'd dreamed of this, here in the moonlight. 'I dreamed of you.'

'And I of you.' Her admission came with razor edges. 'Be careful, Casimir. People break.'

More curses, all his as he buried his head in the curve of her neck and held still. Trembling as she trembled beneath him. It had been like this their first time too. All heat and need, no thought in any of it. She'd borne his child, all alone, and stayed alone afterwards if reports could be believed.

He believed.

'Forgive me.' As he claimed her mouth again and trailed his hand from her wrist down her arm and the hollow of her underarm, around the back of her waist. He lifted her to meet him, centre to centre as she wrapped her legs around him and her arms around his neck. 'Tell me you want this.'

'I want you.'

He pushed in on a groan and smothered her keening wail with his mouth. All the way in until he was buried as deep as he could go, no barrier between them. This wasn't just sex, up here at the top of the world with ancient stone on one side, the valley below and stars looking over them. It never had been just sex between them.

This was devotion.

He began to move, breath harsh and flesh willing, and Ana flowed with him, supple and pliant. They fitted, their bodies completely and effortlessly attuned to each other, and pleasure soared. He'd missed this.

Needed it.

'Please,' he begged, and she kissed him again, giving him everything, convulsing around him and he in turn held nothing back. Not the yearning, the regret or the cruel whip of hunger still riding him.

New plan. We're getting married, he thought.

Gathering her close, and knowing full well that she was still too far gone for speech, he carried her to his bed.

Ana woke with the dawn, aching and pliant. The bed beneath her was unfamiliar but the man beside her wasn't. She knew his touch and the scent of him. The warmth of his skin beneath her cheek and the hills and valleys of his chest. He had a broad chest narrowing to a trim waist and a perfectly curved bottom. He was plentifully endowed, long and thick, and knew exactly how to use that which he'd been given. Last night he'd revealed exactly how well he remembered her lovemaking preferences.

Only man who'd ever been able to make her scream. She'd been so lost in him.

Forget all her scruples and the complications arising. She'd only seen him.

They'd exhausted what their bodies were capable of last night, not surrendering to sleep until the early hours of the morning. Still naked, both. Still craving the connection of skin on skin, as if determined to let nothing come between them.

In the darkness of the night, here in this secluded fortress, it had worked for them.

And now morning was stealing in.

Ana closed her eyes, the better to shut it out, her lips to his chest and her tongue slipping past her lips to taste him. The salt on his skin, the hardening nub of his nipple, oh, she liked that. Enough to fit her lips to the circle of dusky flesh and suck gently.

He woke with a shuddering breath and wound his fingers in her hair. 'More,' he said in a voice still thick with sleep, so she dragged her lips across to his other nipple.

The man had a monarchy to serve and a father to bury. Once dawn broke he would belong to them and not to her and maybe he'd break her heart all over again.

But it wasn't dawn yet.

CHAPTER FIVE

CASIMIR WOKE IN a bed that had seen enough hard use that the bottom sheet had come free of its corners. The top sheet rode low on his back; any other coverings had long since left the vicinity. The bed was a wreck and Casimir was draped across the middle of it, on his stomach.

With Rudolpho and a loaded breakfast tray staring impassively at him.

'What time is it?' he muttered.

'Eleven.'

Eleven? He'd had a meeting with Augustus—*King* Augustus of Arun—and his sister, Moriana at ten in the city. And last night he'd forgotten to tell Rudolpho he wanted to cancel it. 'My meeting—'

'Rescheduled.'

'To when?'

'Two p.m. I took the liberty of deciding you needed to sleep. I am not without eyes or ears, Your Majesty. Or experience when it comes to what people need but won't ask for.'

'You presume a lot, old man.' Even if he was right. Cursing, Casimir rolled out of bed and strode towards the bathroom as Rudolpho set the tray down on the table by the window and opened the curtains to let daylight in. 'Does the press have my tribute to my father?'

'It's been playing all morning. They want more.'

They always did. 'Set up a press conference for Monday at noon. I'll give them everything they never wanted and more. I'm giving Claudia's duchy to Sophia.'

He'd reached the bathroom and the older man had not followed him. The silence was not encouraging. Grabbing a towel, he slung it around his hips and turned back, eyebrow raised as he sought Rudolpho's opinion.

'That's...one way of incorporating her,' Rudolpho said finally, still fiddling with the curtains.

'And I'm marrying Anastasia Douglas.'

Rudolpho stopped dead.

'If you have something to say, say it,' Casimir said.

The older man cleared his throat. 'When?'

'When do I want you to say something?'

'When do you intend to marry this woman no one knows?'

'After the burial. After the coronation. After I claim Sophia as mine. It's the next logical step.'

'Logic,' Rudolpho echoed, and side-eyed the bed. 'Does logic have *anything* to do with this?'

Probably not. But after last night with Ana he felt more at home in his skin than he'd ever felt before, and he wasn't giving up on that without a fight. He could see the future now, in all its splendour. And Ana was an integral part of it. 'You sound sceptical.'

Rudolpho smiled tightly. 'That's what chief advisors are for. What of your relationship with Moriana of Arun? There is an understanding there.'

'Moriana's been in no more of a hurry to marry than me.'

'But she does want to marry eventually. And she's been promised a king.'

He knew it. And he was that king. 'I'll get her another king. Theodosius of Liesendaach.'

He didn't think it possible for Rudolpho's eyebrows to rise any more but they did. 'The wastrel?'

'He's surprisingly reliable. The wastrel image is carefully cultivated.'

Rudolpho wasn't buying it.

Never mind. He didn't have to convince Rudolpho. He had only to convince Moriana. 'Onto more immediate concerns,' he prompted. 'I want Sophia's image in the press restricted as much as possible. She's the innocent in all of this, just as Claudia was innocent of the crimes committed against her. The daughters of Byzenmaach must be protected.'

'That's the message?'

'Yes. Comparisons with my sister will be inevitable. Use them.'

'And the mistress who kept your child from you all these years? The one you now intend to marry? How would you like us to spin *that*?'

Be careful, Casimir. People break.

'We tell the truth. She didn't know who I was because I never told her. We had one week together. I left her to return to Byzenmaach and my duties here. I looked her up recently on an ill-advised whim. Romance ensued. We're madly in love and looking forward to our wedding.'

'*That's* the line you want to spin?'

Casimir studied the older man. 'You don't like it?'

'Not at all,' the other man said. 'It's—'

'Idiotic is the word you're looking for.'

The words had not come from Rudolpho. They'd come from the doorway, and the voice was decidedly feminine. Ana stood there, fully dressed in grey trousers and a scoop-necked black T-shirt that emphasised all her curves. Her make-up was perfect and she'd pulled her hair back into a sleek chignon. The warm and willing woman who'd given herself over to him so completely last night was nowhere in evidence and in its place a mask of cool and steely composure graced her features. He knew such masks well. He used them regularly.

'Marrying you will protect you from the worst of the slander,' he offered.

'What's a little slander to a king's gold-digging mistress? I'll get used to it. Who knows? I might even cultivate it to my benefit. I'm not marrying you.' She sounded quite adamant.

'Why not?'

'Because you didn't ask!' The tirade that followed was rich in a language he didn't know; nonetheless he got the gist of it. 'I will marry for love, Casimir, or not at all,' she said at last, in English. 'And you don't love me.'

'But the sex is good.'

She smiled, fast and reckless. 'I can get good sex anywhere. I don't need your assistance.'

Oh, it was *on*. If she wanted an argument she'd get one. 'Is that so?'

'Count on it. And will you at some point in existence put some clothes on?'

He smirked; he couldn't help it. 'Still distracting, right? Rudolpho, that will be all for now.'

It was a battle for who wanted to get gone faster, Ana or Rudolpho.

'I'm not marrying you,' she yelled from somewhere outside his room, her composure a thing of the past. 'You're a self-obsessed, insufferable lunatic.'

'No, I'm making the best of a bad situation. Lunch at twelve on the terrace,' he yelled back. 'You and me.'

Nothing by way of reply.

'I'll wear clothes,' he offered, and wondered afresh at her capacity to bring out his playfulness.

Still nothing. He stalked to the door and watched her retreat. The rigid shoulders were at odds with the delectable curves of her buttocks. Her sleekly tamed hair a stark contrast to her passionate soul. 'Last night you said that if we made love and I then married another, you would make my life a living hell,' he said to her retreating form. 'I believed you.'

And then the devil rose up and he baited her some more. 'I took it as a wedding proposal in and of itself. Your proposal to me.'

She still didn't look back.

'I said yes,' he added helpfully, and at this Anastasia turned.

'I want a DNA test for my daughter,' she grated. 'She can't be yours. She's too bright!'

'You're right. We *are* going to need a DNA test for Sophia in order to satisfy Byzenmaach. But I'm convinced.'

Her eyes narrowed with deadly intent, a subtle reminder never to put her in charge of a pitchfork.

'Can't talk now,' he said. 'I need to shower. I smell like...' he sniffed at his shoulder '...you.'

'I'm leaving. I'm going to bribe your helicopter pilot with good sex and get him to take us somewhere *you can't go.*'

He sent her an angel's smile. 'Good luck with that. See you at noon.'

The garden terrace, Ana discovered, overlooked a walled garden full of espaliered fruit trees and whimsical flower beds. Surrounded by twelve-foot stone walls and divided by low internal walls that acted as heat banks, it overlooked the stables, and beyond that a narrow mountain pass. Apart from a few scattered outbuildings for animals there were no other dwellings here. Isolation ruled this fortress, no matter how many luxuries they tried to soften it with.

Sophia walked the garden with Lor, collecting hardy herbs and vegetables that grew at this altitude and the wolfhound, Jelly, walked with them, never venturing far. It was the dog's first foray away from her puppies, and Ana had no idea how they'd coaxed her there or whether she walked with them willingly, trusting the safety of her offspring back in the kitchen. It was almost noon, and she'd been waiting for Casimir to arrive for the past ten minutes.

First he demanded she be somewhere and then he didn't show. It was a sign, she decided grimly. How many more signs did she need before she got the message that on a list of his priorities she rated very low?

Marry him and have him run roughshod over her life for evermore? No, no and no.

He came up beside her, his footfall on bleak grey tiles unencumbered by greenery. It was two minutes to twelve and she couldn't even fault him for being late.

'I don't know how you stand it here,' she said by way of greeting.

'What don't you like about it?'

'Apart from the isolation? My inability to leave at any time.'

'It takes all day by horse to get over the mountain pass but it can be done,' he said. 'There's a village on the other side. Or it's half an hour by helicopter to the capital. No time at all, really.'

'*If* you command the helicopter. Or the horse.'

'Fair point.'

He scrubbed up well in dark trousers and a white collared shirt, open at the neck, and dark sunglasses. His version of informal wear, perhaps. And he smelled better than he looked.

'Are you sniffing me?' he asked with a tilt to his lips that said he didn't mind at all.

'No. It's just…the soap here is good.'

'I hadn't noticed.'

'All citrus and woodsy. You're probably too used to it.'

'You weren't in my bed this morning when I woke.'

'Well, I was in it when Lor requested my presence because my daughter was awake and wondering where I was,' she said drily. Lor had been uncharacteristically subdued. Ana had been mortified.

'Were you embarrassed?'

'Yes. It wasn't my finest moment. You bring out the worst in me.'

'And the best,' he said. 'I don't know what you bring out in me. The desire to live a more carefree life, perhaps. Rudolpho thinks I've gone mad. He's never seen this side of me before.'

'You should probably take that as a warning. I'm a bad influence.'

'You might be right. I've scandalised Rudolpho. He's reminding me I have a funeral and a coronation to attend before I can even start thinking about a royal wedding.'

'He seems a sensible man. You should listen to him.'

'He's served my family for forty years.'

'You should definitely listen to him. Before you make a very large mistake.'

'My offer is genuine, Anastasia, no matter what you think. I want to marry you.'

'For convenience.'

'It would be convenient, yes. Byzenmaach has been

without a female role model for a very long time. I dare say they'd welcome one.'

'Yes, and they've been promised one—a proper one. Moriana, isn't it?'

He ignored her question completely. 'You could become that role model if you put your mind to it. Think of it as a new career.'

'No, thank you. I already have a career.' Was he trying to sell her on the role? Because she wasn't buying. 'I don't envy you your status. You can keep your royal trappings.'

'And that's why you'd make a good queen. It's not all bad, Anastasia. Being able to wield influence on a grand scale can be rewarding. You can showcase the causes you're passionate about. Shine a light on situations that need improving. There can be downtime too. Like this morning, for example. Nothing to do. Are you hungry? I'm hungry.'

And lunch was being served. The table had been set when she wasn't looking. The platter of breads, meats, cheeses, pastries and fruit would mean no one left the table hungry. The linen napkins were green with white daisies on them and the flower arrangement was informally whimsical. Her mother would have set a similar table for a casual Sunday get-together, although there'd probably be more salad involved.

He looked towards the table and somehow read her thoughts.

'It's not all formality and perfect table manners,' he offered.

'Who's joining us?' The table was set for three.

'Our daughter, is she not? Don't you usually dine with her?'

Her fault entirely that she'd interpreted his invitation

to mean her alone and not Sophia as well. Sophia was the only reason Ana was here in his presence at all.

There was wariness in Sophia's eyes as Ana approached. So far this morning, she had been having a wonderful time what with no schoolwork to do, animals to tend and Lor dancing attendance on her.

'Lunchtime,' Ana said when she reached them, and Lor looked up and nodded and Sophia looked towards the balcony and frowned.

'With him?'

'Yes. With him.' Was Cas still a prince until his coronation? When did he take the title of king? There was so much about his world that she didn't know.

Sophia took her outstretched hand. 'I don't think he likes me.'

'Why wouldn't he?'

Sophia's hand tightened in hers. 'What if I don't like him?'

'That would be a problem.'

'You don't like him.'

'Not true. I like him well enough at times. Shall we wash our hands at the tap?'

They washed, and then Lor was there with a tea towel in hand so that they didn't wipe their hands on their clothes. They reached Cas eventually and he saw them seated and took the chair opposite both of them. Sophia studied him solemnly. 'Maman says your father is dead.'

Casimir nodded. 'He is.'

'*Dead*, dead or dead like you?'

'*Dead*, dead.'

'Maman says I look like your sister,' Sophia said next.

'You do.'

'Where is she?'

'Dead.'

'*Dead*, dead or dead like you?'

'*Dead*, dead.' He turned towards Ana, a little wild-eyed around the edges. Conversations with morbid six-year-olds could do that to a man. 'And how are your parents?'

'They're very well. We spoke to them yesterday.' He probably didn't want a rundown on the sense of betrayal her parents had felt at not being trusted with her secret for the past seven years. For all their support, they'd never seen her silence as anything but her lack of trust in them.

'Am I going to be a princess?' Sophia said.

'Do you want to be a princess?' Cas glanced up from the act of filling his plate.

'Would I have to stay locked in the tallest tower of the castle and be guarded by a fire-breathing dragon?'

The plate-filling stopped abruptly. 'No. You wouldn't have to do that.'

'Fairy tales,' Ana murmured. 'Always a nightmare.'

'Would I have to stay here?' Sophia regarded him anxiously.

'Sometimes,' he said.

'Maman doesn't want to stay here.'

'I know.' The glance he slid Ana was enigmatic. 'So, for now, perhaps we will have to find somewhere else for you and your *mère* to live, and you can visit me here when you would like to practice being a princess. And when you want to see Jelly the Ninth and Alberto the eagle owl.'

'Alberto the eagle owl?' Sophia regarded her father with owl eyes of her own.

'You haven't seen Alberto the eagle owl yet? He came here when he was very young and sick and didn't know to be afraid of people handling him. Tomas the falconer hand raised him and uses him today to help settle other injured birds that arrive here scared and afraid. He's big, very big, with orange eyes and ears that stick out and can go up and down and sideways and he can hear very well.'

'Does he come when you call?'

'He does. I like that in a bird. But he's asleep now, and I would not abuse my power by rousing him for no good reason. Perhaps later this evening when he is awake we can call him and feed him.'

'Will Tomas be there?' asked Sophia.

'He usually is when it comes to feeding the birds.'

'Tomas doesn't like me,' Sophia announced.

'Oh?' Casimir studied his daughter coolly. 'How do you know?'

'Lor took me to see the hawks in the big cage while Tomas was there and when he saw me he looked like he wanted to cry. And then he didn't look at me again the whole time and then he left and he didn't even say goodbye. Everyone else here says hello *and* goodbye.'

'I see,' said Casimir.

'So he doesn't like me.'

'I really don't think that's the problem.'

Sophia waited for more but Cas had clearly said all he was going to say on the subject of Tomas and his lack of goodbyes. 'Eat,' he said instead, pointing to Sophia's plate, at which point she dutifully pushed a tiny tomato around her plate with a fork.

'What does Alberto the eagle owl eat?' she asked.

'Dead things,' said Cas. 'Preferably still warm.'

'Boy, do you have a lot to learn about father-daughter conversations,' Ana murmured and he smiled, brief but sure.

'I thought I was doing rather well. Staying on topic.'

'Are you sure you don't have a dragon?' asked Sophia. 'Because this would be a good place for a dragon to live.'

'No dragons,' he said firmly.

'Because it could come when you called. Down from the mountains to guard the princess from the evil frogs.'

'Do we have evil frogs?' he asked with considerable calm.

'Yes,' said Sophia. 'They're very big. But they don't have ears.'

Cas silently offered to fill their glasses with juice. 'You can add to this conversation any time you like,' he told Ana.

'Wouldn't dream of interrupting.' It wasn't a regular family conversation, by any means. Ana had no experience when it came to sharing her daughter, and Casimir had no experience with daughters at all, but somehow she was enjoying herself.

They ate. Cas and her daughter talked about all manner of things. From places they'd been to favourite foods to good names for puppies. Only when a butterfly landed on a cake and Sophia held out her hand to attract it did he falter, standing up with an abruptness that made them stare, and sent the butterfly flying off into the garden.

Sophia followed its progress before turning reproachful eyes on Cas.

'Sorry to startle you,' he muttered. 'I need to be...not here. Excuse me.'

'Yes, of course.' Not that he needed anyone's permission to leave, but the man seemed downright rattled. 'Everything okay?'

'Saw a ghost,' he muttered, and Sophia's eyes widened. He looked at his daughter and winced. 'Not a *ghost*, ghost,' he corrected rapidly. 'We don't have ghosts here. At all. Ever. Or dragons. No dragons here.'

'Cas?' Ana murmured.

'What?' He sounded entirely too grateful for the interruption. Lost, for once, as opposed to entirely too much in charge of his world.

'You're making it worse.'

'I know,' he said, a proud man, utterly undone by a small girl.

Ana smiled.

'Not funny,' he muttered.

'Oh, come on.' It was a little bit funny. All that towering helplessness in the face of butterflies and evil frogs. 'Thank you for inviting us to lunch. Great idea. We could do this again tomorrow.'

His eyes widened in dismay. 'I, ah, may have other stuff on.'

'What kind of stuff?' asked Sophia.

'Kingly stuff,' he offered.

Ana grinned. Oh, this was good. 'Do tell us more. Are there donkeys involved?'

She knew with absolute clarity the moment when he fell. When he stopped being a man of duty and surrendered utterly to absurdity. 'No donkeys,' he said. 'Unless you'd like one?'

'I'd like one,' Sophia said, and Ana smiled beatifically. This was too easy. The man needed more practice if he intended to take on her and Sophia both.

'Right,' he said. 'Right. A live donkey?'

Both Ana and Sophia nodded.

'Just checking,' he said. 'I really do need to go and rule…something.'

'Enjoy,' she said. 'And thank you once again for our lunch invitation. Did you have fun? Even with clothes on, I had fun.'

CHAPTER SIX

ANA FOUND HIM in the library later that afternoon. The large walnut table that ran the length of the room like a spine had been covered in newspaper clippings and photographs, some of them yellowed with age. He smiled when she came in and once more she sensed a deep weariness in him that he kept carefully hidden.

'Am I interrupting?' she asked.

'I don't mind. It's time for a break anyway.'

'That's what Lor said. She said you were back from your meeting and sent me to woo you with talk of coffee and something called Borek, which apparently you like.'

'Pastry,' he murmured. 'Predominantly with a meat filling, although you can use anything. Meat pie.'

'Simple tastes.'

'Borek is *never* simple.' Given enough prompting, this man would play. She kept catching glimpses of the man she'd once known, and that man had been irresistible, never mind his secrets.

'Lor says they'll be hot from the wood-fired brick oven in ten minutes.' Lor liked to do things the traditional way here. 'What are you doing?'

'Choosing a photo of my sister to release to the press tomorrow, and seeing what they've already got so that I can better predict what will be regurgitated once they get wind of Sophia. Are there any photographs of Sophia online?'

'No.'

'Good. That's good.'

Ana stepped forward to take a better look at the photographs spread out on the table. She'd read the newspaper articles about his sister's death when she'd first researched him but she hadn't revisited them in years. She picked up an informal photo of his sister in what looked like this very library. The resemblance to Sophia was uncanny.

'The press release I read said your father refused to negotiate with the kidnappers.'

'Correct.'

'What did they want?'

'Water.' Casimir hesitated, as if warring over what to say next. 'There were plans afoot to build a dam in the mountains. It was a good plan for its time but, as always, there was opposition. Villages to be relocated, environmental studies to be done, water distribution rights to be negotiated with the mountain tribes to the north— a proud, fierce people who didn't always suffer my father's rule in silence. My father had been meeting with them. Trying to appease them.' Casimir's lips twisted in mockery. 'That was his interpretation, anyway. He invited their leader to the palace to continue discussions. I remember meeting the man.'

'What was he like?' she asked softly.

'Kind.' The word seemed wrenched from Cas's mouth. 'Kind to a small boy who had forgotten his place and barged into his father's library unannounced. In my defence, I did not know they were there. All I wanted was a book on birds for Tomas. Anyway—' Cas shook himself as if trying to remove the memory from his soul '—

my father and this man fell out and my father refused all water rights for the mountain tribes. Negotiations ceased. Petitions from the north went unread. My father's advisors tried to soften his stance, to no avail. My father was a proud and unyielding man. No one could sway him. People say he brought what happened next upon himself.'

Ana's gaze flicked to the pictures on the table. 'What did happen next?'

'How does one force a man to realise that he's taking away the future of a people?' Casimir said bleakly. 'It's very simple, really. You take away *his* future and you try to make him compromise. But they made a mistake, the people who came for Claudia and for me. They only took one of us.'

'Why?'

'Because they couldn't find me. Such a stupid thing, really. They had someone on the inside, a palace guard, and had chosen their time carefully. It was dusk. We were always allowed to play in the maze garden in the hour before dinner, and dinner was always served at dusk. The kidnappers expected to find me and my sister both. Unfortunately for them, I'd gone to the kitchen to get a jar to put a dragonfly in. Claudia had caught one and wanted to show Tomas before releasing it again. She was a gentle soul, my sister. She was seven years old, I was ten and I should never have left her alone in that garden.'

'Surely no one blamed you?' Ana couldn't comprehend anyone blaming Claudia's abduction on him. 'Where were all the *other* palace guards?'

'Absent. In on it. Diverted from the scene. Take your pick.'

Oh.

'The first ransom demand came within hours. Generous water rights for the mountain tribes in return for my sister's release. My father refused to negotiate. The next demand was accompanied by Claudia's hair. They offered to return Claudia in return for him. He refused. The demand after that was accompanied by Claudia's dress. Me for my sister. My father laughed at that one, and refused them yet again. And then they got creative.' His voice held an echo of old despair. 'That's not common knowledge.'

'Those choices weren't choices,' she said bluntly.

'The first one was. He wouldn't even negotiate. All the recommended procedures. He didn't follow any of them.'

'How do you know that?'

'I was there.'

'You were *ten*. I can't imagine you were included in every briefing.'

Casimir smiled bitterly. You'd be surprised. My father was big on having me learn by example.'

'And what did you learn?'

'That I will never be like him. No matter how hard he tried to mould me in his image, I am my own man. I would have traded water rights for Claudia and to hell with my pride and my fury. I'd have negotiated.'

He stood, head bent, as if staring at the photos and newspaper clippings on the desk, but she didn't think he was seeing any of it. 'What did your mother think?'

'I'll never know. She took to her rooms the day Claudia's dress arrived and reappeared six months later, brain addled and addicted to sedatives. Didn't even manage to get out of bed the day of my sister's memorial service.'

Ana tried to imagine sending Sophia out to face a day like that while Ana stayed in bed and pulled the covers over her head. One child was gone, sure enough, but the other one had been right there and hurting, and very much at the mercy of a ruthless king.

'She wasn't a strong woman,' Casimir offered quietly. 'But I loved her very much.'

God. She didn't know how to comfort this man, didn't think he'd accept it if it wasn't cloaked in sex. But she wanted to help him, truly she did. And she wanted, more than anything, to spirit him away from all of the grief spread out in front of him.

'I've waited a long time for the crown, Anastasia. I aim to create a bright and prosperous future for all of Byzenmaach's children, and if that means dealing once again with my sister's kidnappers I'll do it. If it means admitting how I wronged you all those years ago and offering to do what I can to fix that now, I'll do it. It's not wrong to want to fix what is broken.'

So fierce, this new king for a new age.

So very, very alone.

'I think you should release these three pictures to the press.' She pointed towards three photos that had already been set to one side. 'And then I think you should get someone, or several someones, to put this stuff away. Then I think you should help me wrap Lor's pastries in a picnic basket and take me halfway up the mountain to where the watch fire used to burn. I want to sit on a rock in this Godforsaken place and look around me and see everything there is to see. I want you to show me the beauty in it.'

He looked at her appraisingly, but he didn't say he couldn't do it. 'You'll need hiking gear.'

'I have sandals and jeans. And I'm prepared to make do.'

Two hours and one breathtakingly steep hike later, Ana sat at the edge of the world and watched falcons soar. She was huffing and red-cheeked on account of the thin mountain air, half her hair had slipped its ponytail and was wrapped around her face and her calf muscles would never be the same again, but it was worth it.

Because Casimir was smiling.

She flopped back against one of the huge torch fire supports, closed her eyes and let her breathing return to regular. A royal helicopter sat on a cleared patch of even ground almost a hundred metres below them, and they'd scrambled the last hundred metres to the watch tower. Well, to be fair, Cas had traversed it with the agility of a mountain goat and Ana had scrambled alongside him until at last he'd held out his hand to her. The last part of the climb had been the steepest bit and also the easiest because of that strong, steadying hand with the blunt nails and the coiled strength behind it.

When they'd reached the top and he'd let her go, she'd felt the loss of his touch more than she cared to admit.

Eyes still closed, she scraped her hair back with her fingers and redid her ponytail. When she opened her eyes again she caught Casimir's gaze.

'Okay,' she said. 'Maybe that might have gone a little better with hiking gear.' But they were alone; Casimir's security team had already been up here and pronounced the area clear and then disappeared into the ether. Cas had then flown her up here, just the two of them, because of course he could fly a helicopter just as well as any pilot could—all-weather jacket, aviator glasses, khaki trousers and hiking boots included. 'So where are we?'

'Falconer's Pass,' he said. 'Named for obvious reasons. It's a World Heritage area. Plenty of endangered bird species here. And the watch towers.' He pointed behind her, towards the other end of the pass. 'There's one over there. And there's one up there, on the ridge of that mountain. See it?'

She followed his gaze, shaded her eyes from the sun and nodded, before moving forward and choosing a big broad rock to sit on, close to the edge of the cliff. She wasn't living dangerously on the edge, even if it felt like it, as she sat and drank in the view. 'Do you need pie? I need pie. I *deserve* pie.'

So he slid the pack from his back and sat beside her and spread Lor's picnic offerings on the rock. He withdrew a slim leather-bound book from the backpack as well and set it to one side of the food.

'You brought a book?' Ana paused in the act of stuffing her mouth full of meat-filled pastry, not the slightest bit less tasty for not being warm.

'It's about a hero called Pechorin,' he said and handed it to her. 'I want to hear it in Russian.'

'But the book is in English.' She checked a page of it with the flick of her fingers. 'And you don't speak Russian.'

'Never stopped you before,' he murmured. 'Listening to you translate is very peaceful, for some reason. Except when you get bored and start inserting random commentary in Lithuanian. Which I understand.'

'Hnh.' No point speaking with her mouth full so she waited until it wasn't. 'So what's so good about this story?'

'I don't know. I've never read it.' He picked up a pie and ate it with far more appetite than she'd seen him display at the lunch table.

'Lunch wasn't so long ago,' she said with the lift of a teasing brow.

'Lunch was extremely stressful,' he countered. 'It's entirely possible I ate less than our daughter did. And she ate one tomato.'

'And a green bean,' Ana informed him. 'Sophia snacks in Lor's kitchen—possibly in much the same fashion you do.'

'Oh,' he said.

'Thank you for spending time with her today,' Ana said next. 'She's very curious about you. You're a remote and romantic figure for her at the moment.'

He looked out over the valley below them and frowned. 'That's not…right. That's not who I want to be in her eyes.'

'What *do* you want her to see when she looks at you?'

'I would have her see someone who cares for her welfare and tries to do right by her.'

'What about love? Would you have her see your love for her?'

He cleared his throat. 'You're assuming I know how to show such a thing.'

Maybe she was. 'Give it time,' she offered lightly. 'Maybe it'll sneak up on you.'

'Did you love her from the start?' he asked, and there was a question with no easy answer. She nodded and blinked sudden moisture from her eyes.

'Did you ever not want her?' His eyes were sharp and saw too much.

'You have a lot of questions.' Ragged words to cover a ragged start when it came to Anastasia's feelings for her daughter.

He nodded, but instead of pursuing it he cleared the food away and picked up the book. 'Will you read to me in Russian? For old times' sake?' he asked, and she took the book and he settled back on the rock with his head resting against the backpack and, after a moment, Ana settled down next to him with her head resting against his chest. It was firm and warm and his hand came up to smooth the hair at her temple and the delicacy of his touch made her close her eyes and long for yesteryear.

She opened the book and her eyes and began to read

about a man embarking on a journey. Four pages in, she started summarising in Lithuanian and wore Casimir's sun-spelled objections with a grin.

Ten pages in she started another story altogether. A story only she knew. An answer to his questions. She told it in Russian because it was better that way and because she'd have never been able to tell it in English.

'I discovered I was pregnant six weeks after you left,' she began. 'Nineteen years old with my lover gone, a baby in my belly and all my study plans shot to hell. I couldn't stop crying for what I'd lost and I couldn't stop remembering what we'd found. I was so in love with you. I'd never felt that way before. I was blind with it.'

She turned a page and read the first couple of lines before continuing her own story. 'I tried denial when it came to the baby growing inside me. Maybe it'd go away the same way you went away and I'd smile and be relieved and pretend to have no regrets. It didn't work. My pregnancy continued. At four months I went to the doctor to start proper antenatal care. At five months I told my parents. Your name never came up. Lonely times for me, my friend. Very lonely, with no one to confide in. I think you know that feeling well. Even better than I do.'

She took a breath and turned a page. 'You knew where I lived even if I had no idea how to contact you. You'd made me feel so loved. There was a part of me that still hoped you'd be back. How could you not be back?'

Cas shifted beneath her and Ana paused. But then he settled, his fingertips at her temple again. 'Keep reading,' he muttered.

'I was nine months pregnant when I saw your picture in a newspaper and realised who you were. *What* you were. I was at my parents' house for the weekend and braving their constant well-meaning interrogation. A baby due almost any day and me still refusing to name the father. I sat in the bath with my belly and my memories and cried myself a river because I knew then that you were never coming back.'

She stopped speaking then. The words on the page were too blurry to read.

'Go on.' His voice was rough and drowsy. Or maybe it was just rough.

'I'm looking for the words,' she said in English. 'They're hard to find.'

She turned another page and closed her eyes. 'Hardest thing I've ever had to do, letting you go. Letting the *thought* of you go. The happy family fantasy. Some days I didn't want to get up in the morning. Life would continue on regardless, and I didn't want to be there. Maybe I do know how your mother felt.'

She could feel the rise and fall of his chest, the gentle press of his fingertips against her hair, although the stroking had stopped. Maybe he'd fallen asleep. She switched back to English. 'Are you still listening?'

'I'm listening.'

More English. 'There's not a lot happening in this story. It's very boring.'

'No, it's not.'

She turned a page. 'It's just a description of place. Mountains and a cottage built against a cliff. Bleating sheep and growling dogs, a crackling fire and some smoke-blackened posts. Sounds ominous.'

'In Russian, Anastasia.'

'You are so right. Why is it that things always sound better in Russian?'

'It's your mother tongue; it's comforting. You've heard it since the womb.'

'My mother has a beautiful speaking voice,' she said,

by way of a distraction. 'You'll fall in love with it. People do.'

'You didn't fall far from that tree, did you?'

'I am taking that compliment and basking in it.'

'Good,' he murmured. 'Read.'

She closed her eyes and began to speak.

'You missed the birth. Not that I blame you. I'd have missed it too if I could because it was brutal. And then my baby was born and she was so beautiful and I fell in love all over again in a different way. And I thanked God for her and for bringing you into my life.'

She felt Cas stroking her hair and it soothed her and helped her speak again. 'I got up. Every morning I got up and I studied and took every bit of help my parents offered and I built us a life and I vowed to never regret what happened between us. I *want* to love like that again. I know I can. But it's never quite right with anyone else. And then you come back, offering everything and nothing. A fairy tale life when all I've ever wanted was your love. And for all your fine lovemaking, you've never offered that.'

She stopped speaking and turned the page, tried to read what was written there, and then Casimir's hand curled around the book and closed it as he dropped it on the ground beside her.

'Marrying you makes a lot of sense, I know that. I just don't know if I can do it and not get lost in you again,' she whispered, and then he was kissing her, slotting his mouth against hers and blotting out the sky. He gave as much as he took and he took everything she had and she thought she tasted tears and maybe they were hers.

It was minutes, maybe years, before he released her and lay back down again with his eyes closed.

'We need to leave soon.' His fingers traced the back

of her hand before entwining with hers. His eyes were still closed and his voice was still rough. 'Best we return before dark.'

'Well, we wouldn't want Tomas the falconer to have to send out the owls.' Ana tried for humour and managed stupidity instead.

'You're right,' he said as he got to his feet and held out his hand to haul her up. 'I'd never hear the end of it.'

Casimir excused himself when they got back to the fortress. He made calls he'd been putting off all day and then sat down to work on his speech for tomorrow. He called Rudolpho in to help and if the older man knew Casimir's request as nothing more than a futile need to control events he couldn't control he made no mention of it. He simply loaded Casimir up with work and sat alongside him and worked his own way through a share of it.

Six pm came and went. Lor delivered their dinner on trays.

'You're different around Anastasia Douglas,' Rudolpho said as they ate. 'Less rigid. More relaxed.'

'Sometimes,' Casimir said. More often than not he was a mess.

'Why?'

Good question. Somehow she made him feel lighter. As if the responsibilities he shouldered could potentially be shared. 'I don't know why. She's always had that effect.' He studied the older man's expression but could read nothing from it. 'Ana brings humour and strength to adversity. And brutal honesty, she brings that too. I like being around her. I can loosen my own reins, and know that she can more than hold her own. What do you even call that?'

'A gift,' said Rudolpho.

'I haven't treated her well in the past.' Understatement.

'Then I trust you'll treat her with more care this time.'

'That's it? That's all the advice you have for me on the matter?'

'I'm not a dating advice column.'

Good to see Rudolpho taking Cas's command to speak up so much to heart.

Eight p.m. came and Rudolpho left. When the clock struck eleven, Casimir knew himself for whipped. Pushing too hard. Trying to cover every angle of his upcoming speech to the nation when all he had to do was say what he had to say and follow through on it.

Easy.

He made his way to his bedroom, stripped down to skin and headed for the pool. Ritual or hedonism, he didn't care. He needed this.

He sank into the water of the main pool tonight and made his way to the far end, where the waterfall flowed when the pump was on. When the pump wasn't on and the sheet of water not falling, the area boasted a wide lip, just beneath water level, where a person might rest their arms while pillowing their head on the edge of the pool. He leaned back, stretched out, closed his eyes and tried to will the tension from his body.

He hadn't really expected Ana to be waiting for him. She'd shared his bed last night, refused his marriage proposal this morning, and made him splinter into a thousand pieces up on the mountain, with her telling a story she'd never told before.

Because Casimir spoke Russian now. Not fluently, not without an accent, but he'd understood every word she'd uttered in the language, and he knew now what she wanted from life. What she was really holding out for.

Love.

Above all, she wanted someone to love her and cherish her as she should be cherished.

The main problem, as he saw it, being that he didn't know how to love anyone. He who'd spent so long keeping people out of his heart and his head that he no longer knew how to let anyone in. A man apart. A man alone. A man who ruled.

The boy who was born to be king.

CHAPTER SEVEN

ANA COULDN'T SLEEP. She'd risen from her bed, slipped the wrap someone had left in the bathroom around her nakedness and stargazed from the darkness of her balcony until her memories of hot flesh and ravenous lovemaking had dimmed. She stayed out there, drawing patterns between the stars, until her flesh grew cold and clammy but still her mind was full of Casimir.

Casimir the man, not Casimir the king.

She couldn't get the butterfly from lunchtime and Cas's reaction to it and his conversations with Sophia out of her head. It was as if he'd wanted to connect with her but didn't quite know how. Given his upbringing, he probably *didn't* know how to be part of a family unit, but she couldn't fault the man for trying.

He'd made more of an impact on his daughter than he knew. He was no longer 'that man' or 'the prince' or 'the king' as far as Sophia was concerned. He was Cas who liked owls but didn't like butterflies. At some point he would stop being Cas and become Papa and then it would be *My father said...* and *My father gave me...* A puppy, a pony, a castle.

Tutors, for mother and daughter both. *Heaven help her.*

She couldn't get his stupid marriage proposal out of her head. There was a time when she would have joyfully said yes. She could still say yes. Bury all her doubt and uncertainty and craving for love beneath an avalanche of practicality. Embrace life as a royal consort. Remain wholly in her daughter's life. *Trust* the man to know what he was doing when he'd made his offer of marriage in the first place.

Two weeks, he'd said when he came for them. *A mere two weeks of your time. We can negotiate...* Now he was offering her a place at his side and a marriage that would decidedly *not* be in name only. Forget about her old life. Learn how to be what he needed her to be—mother to a duchess and consort to a king—and maybe one day she'd feel more at home and less utterly out of her depth. Forget those wild dreams of Casimir loving her with all his heart. Instead be content with what he was offering.

Compromise.

The air on the walkway was too crisp. The view was too superb. This walkway was the jewel in the fortress crown, loading her senses until they were raw. The shy moon and the shadows, the lick of air on already cold skin. She thought of Casimir, the man who'd haunted her dreams for years and who'd taken her again last night with a hunger she'd been powerless to resist. When it came to pure passion he would always win.

Whether he offered love or not, she wanted him.

When darkness fell and the world disappeared, she always wanted him.

He was in the pool when she pushed the door to the bath-house open, his head tipped back, his arms spread wide and his legs stretched out before him. Hedonism or crucifixion, she didn't know. All she did know was that she felt his presence like a blow to her already overloaded senses.

He lifted his head to look at her, his eyes dark with

secrets, and he watched in silence as she sat at the edge of the pool and delicately dipped first one foot in the water and then the other. Her robe stayed on, firmly tied at the waist.

For now.

Hot water caressed her feet and ankles and lapped at her calves, but it was Casimir's gaze that burned. She felt it on her skin, on her breasts until they peaked for him, high on her arms, the curve of her shoulders.

She lifted her arms to her hair and bundled it in a loose knot high on her head. It might stay up, it might not; that wasn't the point.

The ravenous heat in Casimir's eyes was the entire point of the exercise.

He tilted his head back to rest against the lip of the pool again and watched her with hooded eyes.

'How are you?' she murmured.

'Today, after lunch with a daughter I don't understand, I angered a princess I was supposed to marry, disappointed her brother who happens to be a neighbouring monarch, and broke a promise I made to my father.' He closed his eyes. He didn't move. 'And then there's you.'

She studied his face in the half light. The arch of his brows, the cut of his cheekbones and the hollows beneath, the sensual generosity of his lips. 'You told Moriana you weren't willing to marry her?'

'Yes.'

'Because of me?'

'Yes.' He opened his eyes and levelled her with his gaze. 'Last night—right here in this room—I chose you. You asked me to.'

She held his gaze, wholly troubled now. 'Words spoken in the heat of passion are often unreliable. Last night I spoke without thinking things through.'

He smiled mirthlessly. 'I spoke true. I would marry you. I want to marry you.'

'Because it's convenient,' she muttered.

'Because it's *more* convenient than any other union I might make, that's true. It rights a wrong. It keeps you wholly in Sophia's life. Isn't that enough?'

'It's kind of only half the fairy tale.'

'Fairy tales aren't real,' he murmured.

But love was. 'What—' she took a deep breath '—what would I have to do if I married you?' She couldn't believe she was even considering it.

'I'm sure someone will have a list.' He smiled again but there were shadows.

'Would there be more children involved?'

'Yes. I need heirs. Legitimate ones. Is that a problem for you?'

'No.' She'd always wanted more children. Likewise, Sophia had always wanted a brother or sister. Or both.

'Would I still be able to work? Outside of official palace duties?'

'Why would you want to?' She had his attention and it burned.

'I've worked hard for my career. I'm proud of it. It helps define who I am. Who I think I am. Without that identity I become…less.'

'Or you could bring those career skills to your new position and become…more.'

'And maybe, just maybe, I'd like to be able to get out of the palace bell jar every now and then. Be me again rather than a creature bound to royal duty.'

'Now there's an argument I can understand,' he murmured. 'It'd be nice to be able to move between worlds and maintain balance in both. I'll not stop you from trying.'

'You don't think it can be done?'

He shrugged. 'I've managed to escape this life and the duties involved exactly once in thirty years. That was when I met you. And I didn't exactly maintain my balance.'

Oh.

'If there's a way to be both king and my own man, I haven't yet found it. Maybe with certain people I can be the man and not the figurehead. Maybe finding balance in a life such as this isn't about the work you do but about the people you allow through. And maybe for you, as royal consort and not born to this life, your experience will be different to mine. You already have another life you can access and I have no objection to you trying to merge the two. Parents, friends, work colleagues— bring them through. *Make* this world work for you. You're strong enough.'

Flattery would get him everywhere.

'Your language skills would be of value to me,' he added wryly. 'Your listening skills would be an asset. You would not lack for political intrigue.'

She looked down past her knees to the water. The picture he'd painted was not an unpleasant one. There were worse lives to be had.

'Would Sophia object to us marrying?' he asked next. 'Is that what's stopping you?'

'No. I don't think she'd object.'

'Then what's stopping you? Because I know you're attracted to me.'

'What gave it away? My unfailing ability to fall into bed with you at a moment's notice or my reduced brain capacity whenever I see you naked?'

'I'm naked now,' he pointed out. 'And you're still thinking.'

'Yes, but not particularly well.'

'I agree. Because you're still saying no to my proposal.' He came to her then, sleek shoulders and silky skin, the water running off him like raindrops down a window pane. Hot hands on her waist, plucking at the tie of her robe before sliding beneath and finding skin. 'Marry me.'

It was hard to stay focused, with his fingers dipping lower and his lips nibbling their way up and over her ribs. 'No.'

'Why not?'

'Because you don't love me.' It was the same answer she'd already given him, only this time it was harder to give. Possibly because his lips had just closed over her left nipple and, oh, he was good at that, sending streaky, jagged slivers of lust through her body. She could feel herself moistening, her legs widening in invitation.

'Do you remember the night we met?' he said as his fingertips drew lazy circles on her skin.

She hadn't forgotten. A shadowy bar and a glance that led to another glance. A smile, the offer of a drink, and then the slow roll of the pad of his thumb across her inner wrist as he'd introduced himself. His fingers had been hard and calloused and he'd been Casimir, just Casimir, and she'd thought him a man who worked with his hands.

He still had them, the calluses.

'I'd never had anyone look at me the way you did,' he murmured. 'No titles. No expectations. Real life didn't come into it.'

'Mine did. I showed you everything.' He'd had a good look around, poked through her hopes, her dreams and then left. 'You lied to me.'

He reached out and caught the fist she'd made of her hand. He stroked her knuckles with the pad of his thumb, stroking her fingers open one by one and then he put her palm to his cheek. His stubble rasped over her skin as he leaned into her touch.

'You rip my heart out every single time,' she whispered.

'Not this time. There are no lies left.' He pressed his lips to her palm and she closed her eyes then and tried not to picture him. All that did was enhance her other senses. The puff of breath against her skin, the touch of his other hand, wet and warm against the back of her neck as he drew her effortlessly closer and transferred his lips to the blade of her cheek, the curve of her jaw and finally, finally to her lips.

He sank into the kiss as if it was the next breath he needed to take.

No words of love from Casimir, King of Byzenmaach, but his body was wide open to her and always had been.

Take it, every line of his beautiful body screamed it, even if he would never say the words. Take *me*.

She led him from the pool and stood him beneath a steaming shower. She towelled him dry, starting at his feet and working her way upwards, peppering his body with kisses while he shuddered and wound gentle hands in her hair and begged for more.

She took him to his bed and made him beg some more until he turned her on her back and entered her, smooth and slow.

'Mine,' he whispered, which wasn't the same as *I love you* and never would be.

'Not yours.' Not even if her body and half her brain said otherwise. 'You can't own people any more. Didn't you learn that at school?'

His grin flashed white in the darkness of the room. 'I didn't go to school. I had tutors.'

'That explains…' She sucked in a breath as his lips grazed her nipple. Whoever had taught him how to worship a woman's body had taught him to excel. 'Your arrogance.'

He withdrew to the point where she feared complete loss, then put his thumb to her centre and slid back in, hard and slow, and made her moan.

'I do allow some people a hearing,' he murmured. 'For example, you could tell me what you wanted me to do to you next and I'd do it.'

The notion that he was hers to command in the bedroom hit hard and made her eyes close. 'I want you to kiss me and keep moving.'

He obliged with a smile, so she buried her hands in his hair and held fast while her body clung and trembled on the precipice of fulfilment.

'See how reasonable I can be?' he whispered against her lips, before stealing her breath.

She broke the kiss and gasped for breath. 'Less talk, more—' She was losing the fight for coherence. 'More.' More of everything.

'Mine.' There was that word again, and there was an implacability about it this time that burrowed beneath her skin like a brand. 'No one else gets to see you like this.'

'Possessive.' She could be possessive too. 'That works both ways.'

'You have me,' he said. 'No marriage to someone else, no heir from anyone but you. That's what you asked for. That's what I've agreed to.'

'I didn't—oh.' A scrape of his fingers across her too-sensitive nipple and the pleasure-pain soared. Maybe she had suggested…something…of the sort. He was kissing her again, the snap of his hips driving her relentlessly towards completion. 'It's not that simple.'

'It really is that simple. I've been thinking about it a lot.'

'Argumentative.' His parents really should have socialised him more.

'Enlightened,' he argued. 'Do you trust me?'

'No.' As he set his teeth to the curve of her neck and bit down hard. 'I'm so close to coming.'

'Do it,' he whispered. 'I want to watch.'

And then she was soaring, clenching, clamping down hard as he surged into her with a muttered curse and began to fill her up.

This was what she remembered most about their time together. The way their bodies talked, no words required. The way he opened up and gave until there was nothing left to give, and nothing more important in this world than being with him.

The morning after began with Ana's groan as Casimir put a hand to her shoulder and tried to nudge her awake. She'd returned to her room in the early hours of the morning rather than share his bed. He'd resented it then. He resented it still, but there'd been no convincing her otherwise. She'd wanted to be closer to Sophia, his daughter, who'd woken with the dawn and was presently keeping Lor and the wolfhound puppies company in the kitchen. Ana had asked to be woken before he left so here he was, keeping his side of the agreement.

An agreement made before he'd realised she'd be returning to her own bed.

How did one wake a woman who didn't want to be woken? Cold water? Brass band? Surely four hours sleep was enough for anyone?

'Press conference,' he murmured as she burrowed into

the bedclothes and tried to make a cave out of them. 'Wake up.'

'More sleep,' she muttered, and then the impact of his words hit home and she sat bolt upright. 'Oh, hell. Press conference.'

'There we go, consciousness. Knew you could do it.'

She spared him a glare from her collection but it was counterbalanced somewhat by the wild tumble of her hair and lips still swollen from greedy kisses through-out the night.

'How is it you look so fresh and rested this morning?' she grumbled. 'You're an incubus, right? You feed off my sexual energy and it gives you enough power to rule the universe.'

'I've had four hours sleep,' he countered, which was more than he'd had in a while. 'And a shower.'

'You do seem rather attached to the whole getting wet thing.' Her gaze started somewhere in the vicinity of his suit trousers and finished somewhere around the shirt collar he had yet to button properly.

'Checking me for marks?' he asked and she shook her head.

'I don't leave marks.'

'Not where people can see them, at any rate,' he murmured, and she smiled a little helplessly. 'I leave for the capital in half an hour, assuming you want to come with me.'

'I do.' She tried scrambling off the bed with a sheet still modestly attached to her person, but gave that up for a bad idea around three seconds later, and headed for the bathroom fully naked.

'Nothing you haven't seen before, right?' she asked over her shoulder as if she knew full well where he was looking.

'Right.' Which didn't stop him from appreciating her nakedness.

'So do I get to be in the audience for this press conference?' she asked next.

'Absolutely not,' he told her. 'It's a circus.'

'I follow politics,' she said. 'I translate for the UN and the floor of the European Parliament. Circuses are my business.'

'But this circus is about you.'

'Exactly why I should be there,' she said. 'And if I am going to be there, where better than in the thick of things? No one knows who I am yet. I can be anonymous.'

She'd reached the bathroom and the last of her words came out muffled. He followed, the better to hear her, or see her, or maybe he wasn't quite ready to put distance between them yet. 'It will be televised. Watch it then.'

'It's not the same. Television coverage will only focus on you. I don't only want to focus on you. I want to focus on the journalists too. The mutterings, the sideways glances. Put me in the room as an interpreter attached to some fictitious international newspaper.' Her hand-waving became more enthusiastic. 'I'll take notes.'

He glanced at her, darkly amused. 'I assume you're expecting Sophia to stay here.'

'Wait—what?'

'Where else would you put her?' he enquired dulcetly. 'In the press gallery too?'

'How about in a nearby room?' she asked.

'No. You're welcome to come with me to the capital, Anastasia, but Sophia stays here.'

'In whose care?'

'Lor's care. Which is where she is now.'

'Why can't Sophia come with us and stay in a nearby

room packed full of security guards while you give your speech and I watch from the crowd?'

'Because she'd be noticed getting off the helicopter and she'd sure as hell be photographed getting back on it.'

'So?'

Ana had so much to learn about image cultivation. He barely knew where to start. 'I don't want to introduce Sophia in person yet. The images we want on the front pages tomorrow have already been chosen by me and vetted by press aides. I know what I want to see and I know how to make it happen. Sophia stays here.'

Ana narrowed her gaze. 'I'm trying to pinpoint exactly which breath it was when you stopped being a… lover and started being an autocratic ass again.'

'King,' he said.

'Mother,' she countered tranquilly. 'You don't *get* to be king when it's just you and me and we're talking about Sophia's movements. We get to be *parents* and make joint decisions.'

'Then, as one parent to another, I'm asking you to consider my words. Your presence at the palace today can be explained away to some extent. You can be part of my advisory team. Sophia can't. She'll be noticed. She's better off waiting here.'

He thought there might more argument to be had but after a moment Ana nodded curtly. 'How long will we be gone?'

'I can have you returned directly after the conference, if that's your preference.'

She nodded again.

'Stop rubbing yourself red,' he snapped. 'What are you trying to do? Wash me away?'

'I'm trying to get clean.' But the ferocious scrubbing stopped and softer soaping resumed. 'I'm just…nervous.'

That made two of them. Not that he could let anyone see his nervousness. Not today and especially not during his inaugural speech.

'Wear your dark trousers and the white shirt you wore the other day and you'll fit into the press gallery easily enough. But you'll stand at the back alongside two of my security people and when they say it's time to go you'll leave without protest. Are we agreed?'

'Do I have a choice?'

'In this, no.' Not when her protection was concerned. 'I need your word that you'll co-operate or I'll leave you behind.'

She'd started scrubbing hard again and this time his hand shot out to stop the abuse of skin. His hands were gentle as he showed her how to wash without scouring but his voice was hard when he spoke again.

'I can't be giving my speech and worrying about your safety at the same time. Give me your word that you'll do what my security team tells you to do.'

'Are you always this paranoid?'

'Always. And not without good reason.'

She couldn't hold his gaze. 'You have my word.'

'We leave in twenty minutes,' he offered.

And left her to it.

CHAPTER EIGHT

ANXIETY RODE ANA hard as the helicopter drew away from the winter fortress. She didn't like leaving Sophia behind, even if she could understand Casimir's reasons for not taking her with them today. Sophia would be cared for here, of that she had no doubt. Her daughter was resilient and seeing Ana leave for work was nothing new.

And still, Ana had never felt such anxiety at the sight of her daughter becoming a speck in the distance.

'She'll be fine,' Casimir said from his seat beside her. He wasn't flying the helicopter today; he'd taken a back seat, alongside her. Behind them sat four security guards. His favourites, Ana thought. His most trusted. The ones who'd been with him before when he came to Geneva, the watchful Katya amongst them.

That had been what…four days ago?

It felt like longer.

Casimir was already dressed for his press conference, or so Ana assumed. Black suit, black tie, white shirt. She was wearing what he'd suggested. Dark trousers, white shirt, a short-cut jacket and low heels. Clothes from a suitcase packed in a hurry, back when they'd agreed she'd only be here for two weeks. She'd kept her make-up to a minimum and scraped her hair into a bun. She'd had twenty minutes to shower and dress. If he wanted her more presentable, he had to give her more time. 'How do I look?' she asked anxiously. 'I didn't bring many clothes.' And she certainly hadn't brought her best clothes. The kind he wore on a daily basis.

'You're beautiful,' he said. 'You always are.'

'I know how to make the most of what I have,' she continued doggedly. 'And I know this outfit is okay for today. That isn't to say that I wouldn't take advice from your people about what to wear, and what Sophia should wear, once you've acknowledged her. Do you have those types of advisors available?'

'Fashion advisors for women? No. It's been a long time since the monarch has needed to dress either a princess or a king's consort.'

'I mean, we have more clothes at home. They're just not *here*. We're only going to be here two weeks, and apart from that I didn't know what we'd need and I still don't know. I know what kind of clothes are acceptable in Geneva—no problem there. I'm just not sure what's acceptable here.' New country, unknown expectations and a public more than willing to crucify her. 'Never mind. I'll figure it out. It'll be fun. Lots and lots of fun.'

'You're nervous,' he said.

'Very.' She clasped her hands together and tucked them between her knees. And not just about clothes. He was about to lay claim to their daughter. There would be no turning back from that.

'I'll ask Moriana to take you shopping. She'll know what's appropriate.'

He sounded serious. He looked serious.

'This would be the Moriana you were supposed to marry, yes?'

'Yes.'

'Yeah, let's not do that.'

'Why not? Do you expect her to hold a grudge?'

'She might.' The woman was losing not just a kingdom but him too. 'How long has she waited for you?'

He had the grace to look slightly discomfited. 'I wouldn't call it waiting on me, as such. Moriana had things to do too. She has a degree in politics and fine arts. Charities to oversee. Her brother's coffers to empty when it comes to the royal family's art collection. She's been busy.'

'Uh huh.' Busy *not* pursuing anyone else, by the sound of things. 'Do you *know* that Moriana's heart isn't involved?'

'I'm sure.'

She wanted to believe him.

'You don't believe me,' he murmured with a half-smile. 'I am very charming, it's true.'

He could be. That was the problem.

Charming. Forceful when he wanted to be. Not to mention confident and assured. 'Are you nervous about the press conference?' she asked.

'I'm not concerned about giving the speech. I'm well prepared. The aftermath could get interesting.'

'Will there be question time?'

'Yes.'

She could only imagine the kind of questions he'd be fielding. 'Good luck with that.'

'Like I said, I'm well prepared.'

Clearly, arrogance could be an asset at times. She looked out of the window at the grey and rocky plains beyond the valley. It was desolate country. Water, or the lack of it, was an issue here. 'If you need a scapegoat today, it's okay to use me. My reputation's disposable.

Blame me for not telling you that you had a daughter if you need to. It's the truth.'

He looked strangely offended by her offer. 'You don't think any of the blame here is mine?'

'That's not what I said.' She looked down and laced her fingers together. 'You have a crown to claim, a monarchy to protect and a daughter to present in the best possible light. They're all important things.'

'And you think *your* reputation's not important?'

'I already have a reputation as a young single mother. People often assume certain things about me because of that. All I'm saying is I don't have a monarchy to lose. You do.' He'd started working on it at his father's side when he was eight years old. 'So be ruthless if you have to. I won't hold it against you.'

He looked down at his own hands then and the rest of the trip passed in silence until a city came into view at the far end of that barren tableland. It was a walled city, medieval in approach. Red roofs and grey stone walls dominated the cityscape and a palace sat clear in the middle of it like the pupil of an eye. There were no skyscrapers—it wasn't that kind of place. There were no big bodies of water. Instead, a series of circular canals ribboned outwards from the palace. What greenery there was looked carefully tended. 'Where does the city's water come from?' she asked.

'A river to the north,' he said. 'Water's precious here. We need more of it.'

'Did you ever build that dam in the mountains?'

'No.' His beautiful lips thinned. 'That project never went ahead. We've a project afoot between Byzenmaach and three neighbouring principalities to jointly address our water shortfall using new technologies and old. I'll be speaking about it today. Selling it.'

'Will it be hard to sell? If it's needed?'

'Ask me tomorrow,' he said with a smile that bordered on mocking.

The royal palace was grander and more ornate than the winter fortress. Soaring spires and covered walkways surrounded a central courtyard big enough to host several football games at once. Ana walked with Casimir and, beyond a curious glance or two from some of the palace staff, no one paid any attention to her at all. They entered an office and the bodyguards stayed outside. Rudolpho waited for them inside the room with a slender file in hand.

'The list of journalists and cameramen attending the press conference,' he said and handed the file to Casimir, who opened the file and began reading.

It was barely nine a.m. and the speech wasn't until twelve. Ana was used to being discreetly present in a room, but never before had she had absolutely no role to play at all.

They *knew* she was there. Rudolpho's narrowed gaze practically eviscerated her. 'I can arrange a private tour of the palace for you this morning, should you be interested.' Polite words to mask her removal.

'Perhaps later,' she murmured. 'Don't mind me. I'm fine where I am for now.' Doing nothing. Feeling wholly out of place and of no use whatsoever. She headed for the bookcase behind the desk. 'I'll read a book on...' she looked closer '...international monetary policy.'

'*I'll* give her the tour.' At last Cas spoke, his attention still on the file. 'Rudolpho, do we have anyone on staff who can function as a wardrobe mistress and fashion advisor to Ana and Sophia?'

'No.' It was an unequivocal reply. Enough to make Cas glance up with a frown for the older man.

'What about the Lady Serah?'

'I can arrange to have the Lady Serah meet with Ms Douglas and Sophia, yes,' said Rudolpho and turned towards Ana. 'His New Majesty may not beg you to leave the lady in question in her current role, but I will. She's my best function planner, has twenty-two years' experience in the role, and her social acumen and statesmanship is unsurpassed.'

Casimir's gaze clashed with Rudolpho's. 'Then I suspect she'll know fashion. Will she not?'

The older man nodded curtly, his gaze dropping to the floor.

'Perhaps she'll be able to recommend someone more suited to a wardrobe consultancy role,' Casimir continued. 'Set up a meeting between her and Ana for today at eleven o clock.'

Rudolpho nodded and left without speaking. Ana watched the advisor leave and shut the door behind him before turning to Casimir. 'What was that?'

'A difference of opinion that has nothing to do with the Lady Serah. When it comes to Rudolpho, I'm all for encouraging outspokenness. It's a slow process but we're getting there.' Casimir seemed unconcerned. 'He's worried about the press conference.'

'You don't have to babysit me if you'd rather concentrate on preparing for that. Like I said, I can read.' She glanced around the room, which looked as if it belonged in the mid-seventeenth century, never mind the computer on the desk. 'Or practice my needlework. Correspond with my parents with the aid of a fountain pen... Plenty to do.'

'Come. We can start with the armoury. It's full of seventeenth and eighteenth-century pieces.'

Of course it was. 'I always wanted to be a knight,' she said.

Ten minutes later she had her head in a helmet and her hand in a gauntlet, trying them on for size. 'They're a little heavy,' she said. 'But otherwise the perfect camouflage and protection required for a spot of shopping in the city, followed by coffee. Then music and dancing, a quick swordfight and then some rutting.'

'Rutting?' he said.

'I'm very earthy. You are too when you're naked. Where's my sword? And yours. You can be my man at arms.'

'Why would I want to be your man at arms when I can be a king?' he countered, but he was pulling a sword from the rack as he said it and holding it out in front of him.

'You'd do it for the freedom,' she said. 'Freedom from service.'

'I'd be serving you instead.' He was surprisingly good with that sword. 'And there would be drudgery.'

'Or you can be a bard. No drudgery, just music. Do you play an instrument?'

'I'd make a terrible bard and I'd starve.' He picked up another sword, swung it and then presented it to her. 'I'm sticking with the king business. It's what I know. All I need is the right queen and I'm set.'

'The poor woman.'

'She won't be poor.'

'She won't be free.'

He frowned. 'That again. What would convince her to give up her freedom for a king?'

'Love.' She kept telling him what she wanted. Over and over, spelling it out for him. 'She might do it if she loved her king enough. And if he loved her back.'

'Kings can't afford love.'

'I don't believe that.' Ana lowered the sword but kept the helmet in place. She needed the protection of him not being able to see her face. 'Love is free. What you can't afford is any more loss.'

He didn't answer. Instead he put his sword back and helped her remove her armour too. 'There are two more places I want to show you,' he said, picking up a jewelled dagger, crossing the room and pushing it into a slot in the wall.

An entire section of stone wall slid aside to reveal a vault with a huge steel door. He stepped up to a control panel, let it scan his right eye and the door clicked open with a hollow whoosh and a light inside came on.

'What is this?'

'This is where we keep Byzenmaach's crown jewels.' Cas opened the door wider and gestured for her to lead the way.

Trepidation at entering a vault warred with deep curiosity as to what she might find on the other side of that door. Curiosity won.

'So how does it work? The acquisition and use of crown jewels?'

'First of all, they don't belong to me; they belong to the monarchy. This, for example, is the crown.' He stopped in front of a crown behind a glass case. 'I'll wear it at my coronation. It's a ceremonial piece and likely won't be seen again until my successor is crowned. We have sceptres, orbs, daggers and rings—each of them a cultural icon with a specific purpose.' He steered her towards another glass case, this one filled with daggers. 'And then there's the jewellery worn by the women of the royal family. Want to see it?'

'Oh, come on, stop torturing me. My appreciation for fine jewellery is alive and well. Of course I want to see it.'

The women's jewellery was kept in steel trays that

slid out at the touch of Casimir's thumbprint on a wall pad. There were trays of rings, trays of necklaces. Tiaras.

'Normally, the royal consort would also have a personal collection held elsewhere but after my mother died, all her jewellery was rolled into the royal collection. Brooches, earrings.' He pressed his thumb to another wall pad and four more trays slid out. 'Bracelets, pendants.'

'Do these have to be worn at specific times?'

'Some do. And of course the more formal pieces are more suited to more formal functions. All have a history that the wearer needs to acknowledge.' He picked up a diamond ring and held it up to the light until it flared a brilliant white. 'This was my mother's engagement ring. Given the state of her marriage and her subsequent suicide, I doubt any monarch will choose to offer it to their future bride.'

'You're superstitious?'

'Maybe a little.' He held it out towards her. 'Would you wear it? Assuming you had agreed to marry me, of course.'

'Which I haven't,' she said. 'But no. I wouldn't wear it.'

He returned it to its velvet-lined spot and picked up another ring. 'What about this one?'

It was an old-fashioned emerald-cut diamond, with a baguette either side. 'It's lovely.'

He picked up her hand and slid it onto her engagement finger. 'It was my great-grandmother's. Sixteen carats and flawless.'

'Uh huh.' She couldn't help but admire it. 'Pretty.' She took it off and gave it back to him.

He put it back, only to put yet another ring on her finger. This one was a brilliant cut stone that flashed intensely pink in the light. 'My grandmother's pink diamond. A gift from her husband on their fiftieth wedding anniversary.'

This one was beyond beautiful. The pink colour giving it a warmth that the others, for all their brilliance, simply didn't have.

'Which do you prefer? This or the one before it?'

She looked at him sharply. 'Are we shopping for an engagement ring?'

'Of course not. Apparently I'm not getting engaged.' His wry smile could have cut these diamonds. 'I'm showing you the royal collection.'

She studied the ring again and couldn't help but admire the way it flashed and the elegant simplicity of the design. 'It's very beautiful,' she said and then took it off and handed it back to him. 'Thank you for the tour.'

He moved to another tray and picked up a necklace set with diamonds and large sapphires, with the biggest sapphire of them all hanging pendant style, as the centrepiece. 'Try this.'

'What? No!'

'C'mon. I'm offering. Your appreciation for fine jewellery is alive and well, remember?'

He took her hand and led her to the end of the row and turned her around so that she stood directly in front of a full-length mirror. He stood behind her while he fastened the necklace around her neck, and the stones were cold but his fingers burned.

'Oh, wow.'

He dealt deftly with the first button of her shirt and then the next, before pushing the collar aside with his fingertips. By the time he was done and her shirt was half hanging from her shoulders, her nipples were erect and his heated gaze was not on the sapphires.

'Stunning,' he murmured. 'The Connaach sapphires have never seen such a setting.'

'They have a name?'

'They do. There are earrings, a pendant and a tiara to match. They date back to the time, and the Court, of Marie Antoinette.'

'That's…very impressive. Take it off.' His gaze met hers in the mirror.

'They're not the first thing I see when I look at you,' he said.

'What *do* you see?'

'Strength.' He slid the necklace from her neck, dragging it low across the swell of her breast first. 'Passion.' He settled her shirt back into its proper position. 'Loyalty.'

She rebuttoned her shirt while he put the necklace away and made the trays of jewellery slide back where they came from.

'You never took a husband,' he said. 'You've had no long-term lovers these past seven years. Why not?'

'You think I stayed alone out of loyalty to you?'

He turned and warily watched her approach. 'I don't know.'

'Have you had lovers these past seven years?' she asked.

'Yes.'

'So have I.' His expression darkened and Ana shrugged. 'Nothing serious, it's true. But I'm open to the idea of walking through life with the right person at my side. I never shunned that thought.'

'But you shun me.'

'You don't love me.'

'But I care about your wellbeing. And there's passion between us. Respect for each other's needs. I've promised you my loyalty. What kind of love do you *want*? Explain it to me.'

He was opening up another sliding tray and picking out a pair of black cufflinks.

'I want the kind where two people stand at each other's side in the middle of this huge and crazy world, with every option known to man open to them, and they know, without a shadow of a doubt, that there is no other place they'd rather be. Love is not an intellectual puzzle. It's a feeling.'

He pocketed the cufflinks. 'Thank you for explaining.'

'You don't understand, do you?'

'I do understand. I've just never felt that way.'

'I know. Why do you think I keep refusing you?'

His smile didn't reach his eyes. 'Could have been any number of reasons. Or a combination of reasons. I like to think that by talking about it with you I'm narrowing it down. Come. I want to show you something else.'

'*More* treasure?'

'Of a sort. This one's practical.'

It took them five minutes to get out of the palace building and another ten to walk through the garden and down the vast expanse of lawn to the southern end of the palace grounds where a two-storey stone building stood. It wasn't small. A dozen huge windows ran the length of both floors, and the lower floor also displayed climbing roses of deepest apricot on its walls. Lavender lined the pathway that ran the length of the building and the garden beds here were the most impressive yet—stuffed full to overflowing with shrubbery, more roses, rosemary, thyme and other more tender herbs.

'This is a cook's garden,' she said, breaking off a tip of lavender and putting it to her nose.

'Yes. It serves the palace kitchen. My grandmother

used to live here, the one whose ring you preferred. She was very fond of her garden. The dower house also has the advantage of being situated within the palace grounds but fully separate from the palace itself.' They reached the corner of the house and turned into the shade of the building. 'I'd like you and Sophia to consider living here on a permanent basis.'

'Excuse me?'

'They duchy I plan to give Sophia is some distance from the capital. This is a better living option for you both, although you will, of course, be free to visit the duchy from time to time.'

'It's too big.'

'I will, of course, pick up the running costs and ensure you have all the staff you need. Some of the rooms are small, if I remember correctly. I don't remember my grandmother's house being austere.'

He took her through an iron gate and into a walled vegetable garden full of fruit trees and nursery plants. Definitely not austere, this part of it. It was kind of frenzied and haphazardly organised. A mixture of old and new and everything in between. But thriving. And there were bees. Probably royal bees.

'The gardeners use this as a plant nursery. It seeds the palace gardens. All this would move somewhere else, of course, were you to accept the offer. And there's the conservatory. Also used by the ground staff and gardeners.'

The conservatory was a huge glass semicircle extending from the house and bursting with greenery. 'The house was mothballed when my grandmother died.' He pulled out a brick that formed part of the wall beside the doorstep, stuck his hand in the hole and pulled out an old-fashioned key.

'Seriously?' she said. '*That's* your security?'

'Needs updating.'

It was clean inside the house, dark but not damp, and as Cas started opening curtains and taking covers off the furniture Ana began to see the appeal. The house was far too big for two people but the common rooms were lovely and the bedrooms were of a size that people wouldn't get lost in.

She opened the door to an ancient bathroom, beautifully tiled in saffron and gold, with a circular bathtub big enough for two. A skylight hovered over it, the same size and shape as the bath. 'This world of yours...it's a little opulent.'

He stood in the doorway, arms folded across his chest, watching her as she took it all in. 'You like it. It reminds you of the bathhouse.'

It did remind her of the bathhouse. 'I could fill it with exotic dancers. You could have a harem.'

'You're tempted.'

'Don't be smug.' But he was correct. If he really was looking to incorporate Sophia into the royal family, this would be one way to do it. A way that allowed Ana some autonomy. From him.

'You could turn some rooms into a business centre. Build a business from here. The house already lies within the palace's security parameters, which makes me very happy,' he offered quietly. 'It would make my security team happy. It would save money.'

'What about my life in Geneva?'

'Anastasia.' He looked torn. 'That life is gone. I'm trying to give you choices. That's not one of them.'

Up until now she'd resisted truly digesting that notion. This house, this fresh new *option*, was forcing her to.

'I'm sorry,' he said.

'No, you're not.' Anger had to be directed somewhere.

'Believe me, I am. I know the value of freedom, even if I've never had it. I can hear in your words and your voice the value *you* put on it. I'm trying to make it up to you.'

'With things.'

'Yes. With things. Useful things. Pretty things. Things that may be of value to you, going forward. Opportunities.'

He turned away to stare towards the bathroom door. 'I'll be moving into my father's old quarters in the summer palace soon. The Byzenmaach monarch resides at the summer palace. Tradition demands it.'

'Even though you prefer your winter fortress?'

'Even then. And even though I would live nearby, you would have complete privacy. This would be your home. I would not venture here uninvited.'

He wanted her to say yes to this. He couldn't hide it. Not with his words and not with his eyes.

'Show me the second floor,' she said.

The second floor was even more inviting than the first, full of sunshine and windows and intimate corners. He took the covers off the sofas and the sideboards in the living room and unrolled the floor rugs and a little more grandeur crept into the space. She could make it less daunting, more lived in. It was indeed an option she could work with. A place from which to learn how best to navigate his world.

Ana looked through a couple more rooms, and Casimir said nothing. A muscle flickered in his jaw. 'We're going to need a couple of wolfhounds,' she said.

'Done.'

'And the gardeners can stay, provided we have full garden access and get to sample the spoils on a random basis.'

He smiled, just a little. 'You will never be without flowers or fresh produce again.'

CHAPTER NINE

THE ROOM THE press conference was to be held in had a podium, several centuries' worth of royal portraiture, and standing room for around one hundred people and their equipment.

Ana stood at the back of the room, not quite a part of things, not quite an outsider. A palace pass graced her neck, two security guards hovered within reach and exit strategies had been discussed. When told to leave by Security, she would leave. She'd given her word.

So far, the press people in the room had barely spared a glance for her. One or two had glanced her way a second time and their gaze had slid to her press tag. Today, she was an employee of Associated Press TPR. Whoever they were.

And then Casimir entered and strode to the podium and silence fell. He looked out over the room and paid her no more attention than anyone else, even though he saw her. He wore a stern and solemn expression and she wondered if he knew he looked older than his years.

He probably did.

If she'd learned anything in the previous half-hour in Casimir's office, with Casimir running through lines of his speech and Rudolpho peppering him with insulting questions, while yet another aide brushed his suit and fastened the cufflinks Casimir pulled from his pocket and handed to him, it was that Casimir and his entourage were consummate professionals.

Only when Rudolpho had presented Casimir with a ring to wear had Casimir faltered.

'It's been resized,' said the older man and Casimir nodded and slid it on his finger without another word and went back to running lines. But he fisted his hand and rubbed the thumb of his other hand over the ring until Rudolpho stopped with the questioning in order to stare pointedly at the offending behaviour.

Casimir scowled, but the ring-rubbing stopped. 'I'm ready,' he said.

Casimir started his speech with a tribute to his father. He talked political achievements and ongoing projects. Ana had heard variations on this speech a thousand times in her capacity as a translator, but it was nicely done and spoke of stability and the alignment of vision.

'I want to talk about water next,' he said and the reporters collectively moved forward. 'For a number of years now, I've been in talks with our neighbouring monarchs—Augustus of Arun, Theodosius of Liesendaach and Valentine of Thallasia. We propose the construction of a water supply system that weaves its way across many borders and regions. It is intended to supply all those in need and the water-harvesting techniques and recycling plants will be at the forefront of technology. As an individual nation we could not afford it, but together with Arun, Thallasia and Liesendaach we can make it work and reap the benefits. Detailed plans are in the press kits available to you as you leave here today and there's one part of the plan that I want to emphasise, beyond all measure.' He took a breath and his jaw seemed to harden. 'No matter who you are, no matter where on our borders you live, no matter what you've done in the past, I invite you to the negotiation table. Your presence is welcome, your opinions are welcome, and your water needs will be considered.'

He paused and looked out over the gathering, as if to let his words sink in. 'I do not dwell on the past. I will not sit back and let fear and hatred rule this monarchy. For the sake of your children and mine, it's time to move forward.'

'Did he just invite the northern mountain tribes back to the negotiation table?' Ana heard one reporter mutter to his cameraman.

'Yep.' The two men exchanged a glance that spoke of deep concern.

'Leonidas will be turning in his grave,' the first one said.

Personally, Ana would rather see Leonidas of Byzenmaach burning in hell for his sins, but maybe that was just her. She shifted from one foot to the other and kept her mouth shut as Cas began to talk of family next.

He talked of his sister and dark days indeed and he spoke of his mother. As pictures of them came up on the viewing screen behind him, he spoke to them. Sometimes with joy, sometimes in sorrow. Always with utter sincerity.

He was good at this.

And then a picture of Sophia appeared. 'I mentioned earlier that I would see old animosities die for the sake of Byzenmaach's children,' he began. 'This is my daughter.'

Ana recognised the park in the background and the clothes Sophia was wearing. The photo couldn't have been more than a week or so old. But Ana hadn't taken it. She crossed her arms over her chest defensively, set her mouth in a firm line and wondered what other surprises this speech of his would bring.

Cameras clicked like crickets at dusk as Casimir continued. 'Her name is Sophia Alexandra, she was conceived seven years ago and I am very, very protective of her.'

Another photo went up—another picture of Sophia. 'As you can see, she bears a strong resemblance to my sister. Sometimes...' he cleared his throat and his gaze sought Ana's '...sometimes she takes my breath away with a gesture or a look that I remember from another time. It hurts my heart and I have to remind myself to look forward, not back. At the same time I can tell you that there is no better motivation for wanting peace and understanding between neighbours than having this child in my life.'

Another picture, this one showing Ana from behind and Sophia at the school gate. Where had he got these pictures? Why hadn't she realised someone had been taking them? Ana felt a twitch between her shoulder blades, as if someone had painted a bullseye on her back.

'My daughter has lived a sheltered life away from the press. Her childhood has been a happy one, and I would see it continue. Any attempt at invasion of her privacy will be met with a security force some may consider excessive. My reply to this is simple. Consider what Byzenmaach—what I—have lost.'

There was one more picture of Sophia, spreadeagled on the floor with Jelly the wolfhound and the little black puppies, her ponytail sloppy and tilted to one side as she oversaw the feeding. Jeans, no shoes, a faded blue Tee—a little girl in all her innocence. The setting showed a stone floor and walls that gave nothing of the location away but hinted at age and grandeur. Protection of the young. The picture was perfect.

He glanced down at the podium and smiled wryly. 'I know you'll have questions and have anticipated some of them. Ladies and gentlemen of the press, the mother of my child is fluent in six languages—including ours—and is an interpreter for the European Parliament and the United Nations.' He touched the ring on his hand briefly, and Ana wondered whether he did so for luck or for courage, or whether the gesture was a totally unconscious one.

'Until now, my daughter and her mother have lived independently of the Byzenmaach monarchy. That is about to change. My daughter will soon begin to take on the roles assigned to her as a valued member of this royal family. She will occupy the duchy formerly held by my sister and will henceforth be known as the Duchess of Sanesch. I thought it fitting. Any questions?'

Oh, dear Lord, were there questions.

Was he married?

Had his father known of the girl?

What of his relationship with Moriana of Arun?

Casimir, King of Byzenmaach, smiled grimly and began answering the questions that suited him.

No, he was not yet married.

Relations with Moriana of Arun were amicable. He had enormous respect and admiration for the princess but marriage was unlikely.

Ana saw sideways glances and raised eyebrows at that one.

The questions continued, a mad jumble of sound with the occasional moment of breathless silence while everyone waited for his answer.

'Are you serious about resuming water negotiations with the very same people who murdered your sister?'

'Yes.'

'When can we see the child in person?'

'When I see fit.'

'What is your relationship with the mother? Do you ever plan to marry and have legitimate heirs? What good is a bastard daughter?'

That last one caused consternation, both within the press and the royal aides assembled. A line had been crossed, a challenge issued. Casimir's fierce hawk eyes turned predatory.

He stared at the reporter who'd dared ask the question. He let the silence build and the reporter squirm for a very long time.

And then he let his displeasure fill the silence just that little bit more.

'This *illegitimate daughter* you shun so quickly is a gift,' he offered finally in a voice that dissuaded argument. 'She has many names in my household—Sophia, Little One, Beloved. *Bastard* is not one of them.'

More buzz from the press at that.

'If history teaches us anything, it is this,' Cas continued. 'It is no easy task to stand beside a king and risk public crucifixion on a daily basis. It is no easy task to live with the constant threat of violence against your own self or your loved ones. The strength required to do so is enormous. Yet here I stand, your king, asking a child in all her innocence to do exactly that. To stand at my side and believe that I can keep her safe. To make her world a better place. Make no mistake, I will see it done.'

Ana's bodyguard touched her arm, albeit briefly, and glanced towards the rear door of the room, before heading towards it. Ana followed reluctantly. She'd given her word. Another security person, this one a man, fell into step behind her. They stopped at the door itself.

Half in, half out, allowing her a view of Casimir still. Casimir caught her gaze and held it for a heartbeat. And then he turned back towards the screen.

A new photo came up, a shot of Ana. Make-up-free and with her hair piled high atop her head in a messy ponytail reminiscent of Sophia's, she wasn't looking straight at the photographer, but rather appeared to be staring intently at something in the distance. Ana tilted her head and tried to place the background. The park in Geneva, near where she lived? No. The walled garden at the winter palace? Ana frowned. The cloistered walkway? Yes.

'There's one more person I'd like you to meet. Not in person today, but soon. Her name is Anastasia Victoria Douglas. She's twenty-six, of English and Russian descent, the mother of my child, and one of the strongest women I know. Which is good news for me and for Byzenmaach. A strong royal consort is a blessing for all.'

Cas looked her way again and a flicker of some undefined expression crossed his face. Sorrow? Apology? *Royal consort? What was he doing?*

'We will be married within the year.'

A picture of two children racing through a garden came up on the screen, a huge wolfhound loping alongside them, and for a moment Ana would have sworn the girl in the picture was Sophia. But it wasn't Sophia. It was Casimir and his sister.

'He's finished,' murmured the bodyguard. 'Go.'

The door closed behind them and minutes later Ana was back in Casimir's office, with the bodyguards stationed just outside. Casimir joined her not thirty seconds later and shut the door behind him.

Ana took one look at him and felt her self-control shatter. 'What was that? What the *hell* was that?'

'Necessary.' Casimir wasn't in the mood for criticism. He'd done what he had to do. He'd gambled it all.

For a woman who looked alarmingly pale, her voice certainly seemed to radiate a lot of heat. 'I *refused* you. In what world does *no* translate into *I'm marrying you within a year*?'

'You're not indifferent to me, Ana.' Surely she could do him the courtesy of admitting it. 'You could come to love me. You're already halfway there.'

'I know that. You know that. *Every man and his falcon at the winter fortress knows that.* Doesn't mean I said yes.' She started pacing and he leaned back against the edge of his desk and watched her work off some of her temper.

'You gave me permission to destroy your reputation in order to preserve mine.'

'Still not a yes!'

'It was a foolish offer and I refuse to do it.' He crossed his arms, trying to get a read on the extent of her distress but she wouldn't stand still long enough for him to properly see her face. 'I want my people to value and protect you, Anastasia. I want stability for Sophia. This is the way to do it.' He drew the ring she'd admired from his pocket and held it out to her.

'No,' she snapped. '*Hell*, no.'

'You liked my mother's ring more?'

'Casimir, I'm not doing this.'

'You want love as well,' he said. 'I'm getting there. I'm willing to work towards it.'

'It's not *work*,' she grated, and then his office door opened and Rudolpho stormed in.

'What the *hell* was that?' the older man said, and then his gaze took in Ana and the ring and he paled. 'God have mercy. You haven't asked her yet?'

'I'm doing it now.' Obviously. 'So if you'll excuse me, I'll get on with it.'

Rudolpho closed his eyes and put both palms to his face. He let out a laugh that sounded ever so slightly hysterical and then wiped his face. 'Your Majesty, I've known you since you were a baby. I've bounced you on my knee. I taught you everything I know about statecraft. And less than a week into your reign you invite the northerners back to our table and announce a wedding when you haven't secured the bride yet? Are you deliberately trying to end your reign? Because I *know* I taught you better than this.'

But Casimir was done with statecraft. 'For thirty years I've been a perfect puppet for this country. No more. I know what I stand for and I know how I want to proceed. I've made my choices very clear. Now all I have to do is get everyone else on board with the plan.'

Rudolpho shook his head. 'You do realise you risk being exiled?'

'We'll see.'

'You could have at least told me what you planned to do today. I thought you were dropping one bombshell. The existence of your daughter. You dropped *three*.'

'I concede that announcing my wedding may have been a mistake.'

'And your plans for the dam?'

'Not a mistake.'

Rudolpho's bleak black gaze encompassed them both. And then he turned on his heel and left.

Casimir sighed heavily.

'Casimir, what are you doing?' Ana asked almost helplessly. 'You're running roughshod over people! Including me! You can't *force* people to do what you want them to do.' She put her hands to her cheeks. Then she crossed her arms in front of her defensively and tucked her hands beneath her armpits. 'I'm not marrying you within a year.'

This really wasn't going according to plan. 'But you will if I fall in love with you. I'm already halfway there.'

'You are nowhere near there!'

He ventured closer, stopping only when he stood in front of her. Close enough to see the sweep of individual eyelashes and the panic in her eyes. 'Hand,' he said and took her fingers in his and raised her knuckles to his lips. She stared daggers at him but she let him do it.

He turned her hand over and placed his lips to her palm before placing his grandmother's ring in it and closing her fingers over it. 'Keep it,' he said. 'It's yours now. Whether you wear it or not.'

'I'm not wearing it.'

'Have a little faith in me,' he said. 'You were right when you said I can't afford any more loss. I'm not losing you again. Therefore I'm going to love you the way you want to be loved.'

'I admire your resolve, Casimir. It's outstanding. But let me repeat something I said to you before. *Love is not an intellectual puzzle!'*

A brief knock on the door announced the arrival of Rudolpho, phone in hand. The chief advisor's gaze swept over them, sharp eyes missing nothing. 'You're not engaged yet,' he said flatly.

'Not yet,' Casimir said blandly. 'But I did give her the ring, should she ever wish to wear it.'

'Excellent, Your Majesty. No engagement and a royal heirloom worth millions lost to a foreigner.'

'Who's on the phone?'

'His Majesty Theodosius of Liesendaach requests that you take his call,' Rudolpho said, heavy on the pomp and ceremony. 'His Majesty Theodosius said, and I quote,

"Put that moron who just screwed Moriana over and stole my bad-boy crown on the phone."' Rudolpho relayed the message with unadulterated pleasure. 'I gather he watched the live broadcast.'

Cas smiled fierce and free. 'Excellent.' It wasn't the response either Rudolpho or Ana had been expecting if the worried glance they shared with each other was any indication. 'Rudolpho, see to it that Anastasia gets back to the winter fortress this afternoon. She's had enough.' Cas turned to Ana next. 'Unless, of course, you need more time for wardrobe meetings. How did that go?'

'Badly,' she said. 'Thank you for asking.'

'I've arranged a secretary for her,' Rudolpho said. 'One of my best.' *You owe me*, the older man's tone suggested.

'I also gave her the dower house,' Cas said. 'It'll need to be staffed and made habitable.'

'Of course, Your Majesty.' A muscle in Rudolpho's jaw twitched. 'Anything else you'd like to give her? Your kingdom? Saturn? Or may I get back to putting out all the *other* fires you've lit?'

'By all means, put them out. I'll even help.' He turned to Ana. 'I'll find you later.'

She glared at him. 'And Rudolpho and I will find you a therapist.'

She swept from the room, with Rudolpho right behind her, but she kept the ring. It was right there in her tightly clenched fist.

Casimir ran a hand across the back of his neck, his body thrumming with the aftermath of freefall. He'd planned for this. Maybe not all of it but most of it. Squaring his shoulders, he lifted the phone to his ear.

'Theo, my old friend. You saw the show?'

'I did indeed. A six-year-old daughter born out of wedlock and a future Queen Consort no one's ever met? I can't top that. It's going to take years.'

'Don't forget the water management plan.'

'Yes, let's not forget the only thing I did know about beforehand. Talk about burying the lead. I'll be on camera within the hour, endorsing the bold new regional plan and congratulating you on your upcoming nuptials. Which… I have no words other than: I hope the hell you know what you're doing. And how's Moriana? Is she even speaking to you right now?'

'About that. I was thinking you could ask her to Liesendaach to—'

'No.'

'—value the royal art collection.'

'I know exactly what my collection is worth. Why do I need the harridan's opinion?'

'You don't. But she needs a face-saver, and you're—'

'Egregiously reckless, feckless and immature. Her words, not mine.'

'I was going to say available,' muttered Casimir. 'And kind-hearted.'

'Debatable,' his childhood friend said drily.

'So what if you and Moriana fight a little?' They never stopped. 'You like it. It keeps you battle-honed.'

'And perpetually wounded.'

'One photo of you looking smitten with her. That's all she needs.'

'That is not what I need.'

'I don't want to see her take a public press battering over this.'

'Well, I'm sure that could have been avoided had you not to all intents and purposes been practically engaged to her *for the past twenty years*. Damn you to hell and back, Casimir, what were you thinking? Do you think it's been pleasant, her having to wait on your whim? She was relying on you to come through for her.'

Cas looked at the phone. He'd heard similar from Augustus, but Augustus was Moriana's brother and naturally protective. Theo, on the other hand, was traditionally not in Moriana's corner. Not ever. 'Hello? Is this Theodosius, despoiler of women? Because for a moment there I thought I was talking to someone who cared about a woman's feelings. Someone deeply invested in the fact that their only female friend of over twenty years might be hurting.'

Silence, then, 'Screw you. You were perfect for her. The golden couple. You never put a foot wrong and now this.'

'She's not broken-hearted.' Casimir tried again. 'I've spoken to her and she's angry, yes. Resentful, yes. Not shy about voicing her displeasure at being made to feel like a fool. But we've never been intimate, not once in all these years.' And that was more than Theo ever needed to know about Casimir's relationship with Moriana.

The silence on the other end of the phone was deep enough to drown in.

'Seriously?' Theo said finally. 'What are you, a monk?'

'Compared to who? You? Yes.'

More silence, and then, 'I'll ask her out. She will refuse and then I'll be done with it.'

'Thank you.'

'You're welcome. Hey, Cas—' Theo's voice had softened '—we're finally doing it. All those years. All our plans.'

'I know.'

'Asking you to offer the northerners a seat at the negotiating table was a big ask, but you did it. I've never been more proud of you. I've never been more proud of anyone.'

Casimir rubbed at his chest to ease the sudden tightness there. 'Thanks.'

Theo cleared his throat. 'Anyway. I'm hanging up now, you ungrateful cur. Some of us have work to do.'

'Call Moriana.'

But he was talking to a dialling tone.

Forty minutes later, Casimir put the phone down and headed for the outer offices where Rudolpho and various other royal aides held court. 'You all saw Theodosius's press conference?'

Everyone nodded.

'Augustus of Arun will follow within the hour, as will Valentine of Thallasia,' he told them. 'It's all been scheduled.'

'What of the north?' asked Rudolpho, his eyes sharply assessing.

'I've had no communication with the mountain tribes to the north,' he said. 'They heard of the new water plans when you did.' He glanced at the clock. 'I don't know if or when we *will* hear from them. Tomorrow I'll send them a formal invitation to negotiation talks here at the palace and ask them to nominate a representative. See if that encourages a reply.'

Rudolpho sighed heavily.

'You disagree with my strategy?' Casimir asked coolly.

'I know who we're likely to get by way of an envoy.'

'You liked him well enough once.'

'That was before I knew what he was truly capable of. You'll barely be able to guarantee him safe passage.'

Rudolpho was right. 'Then he can come to the winter fortress, where I *can* guarantee safe passage.'

'You would put him within a mountain range of your daughter? Of your future wife?'

'I'll send them elsewhere.'

The older man sighed again. 'There's no dissuading you from this course of action, is there?'

'I'm fully committed. I have been for years.'

'You planned this. You and Liesendaach, Arun and Thallasia. When?'

'Years ago. Back when we were young men dreaming big.'

Rudolpho stiffened. 'Why didn't you *tell* me?'

'You would have been duty-bound to tell my father and he would have destroyed any fair hope of these plans ever gaining traction.'

'Your father's been dead for four days. You could have told me what you planned to do during the hours and hours we spent working on your speech last night. A speech you *did not give.*'

'I gave parts of it.' But his chief advisor was right. 'I could have told you my plans. I chose not to.' Casimir looked around the room at the other aides, some of them pretending to work, others not bothering to hide their avid interest in the conversation. 'I've been waiting years to right old wrongs and if you think I haven't planned these next few days and what needs to happen in order to gain the confidence of my people down to the second, you're wrong. Theo, Augustus and Valentine will stand with me because it benefits us all. Formal letters of invitation to peace talks will be sent north.'

He stood tall and squared his shoulders. 'You know me. For thirty years I have stood at my father's side and been what he wanted me to be. What Byzenmaach needed me to be. I have served. I have learned from my father's mistakes. And I will not let my country stagnate and fail any longer. If you don't like my vision for the future, if you are not capable of dealing fairly with those I bring to the table, there's the door.'

No one moved.

'Right,' said Rudolpho. 'Let's get to work.'

Ana returned to the winter fortress just in time to catch the afternoon news and a replay of Casimir's speech. She watched it with Lor, who had a faintly proud smile on her face and nodded when it was done.

'Congratulations on your engagement,' Lor said, but Ana was already shaking her head.

'I'm not… We're not…engaged. I didn't agree to that. Casimir made a mistake.'

Lor said nothing.

'But the rest of it was good,' Ana said in a small voice. 'Excellent. He's an accomplished statesman.'

'Your mother phoned while you were at the palace,' Lor said. 'She too offered her congratulations.'

Ana winced. 'I should probably call her back.' She sent Lor a wan smile and figured she should probably call from the privacy of her room.

'Ana.' Lor stopped her at the door. 'Ms Douglas.'

'I thought we'd moved past Ms Douglas,' Ana said.

'He's a good man.' Lor twisted her hands in her apron. 'He was a good boy. Loyal to a fault, even when his emotional needs were not being met. And they were very rarely met. He might not show it, or say it, but he cares for you and the little one. I can see the change in him.'

'He doesn't know love,' Ana said. 'He doesn't know how to let anyone in.'

Lor lifted her chin. 'Then teach him.'

Love wasn't something that could be taught, decided Ana as she walked into her room and picked up the phone.

Manners could be taught. Languages could be taught. But love was different.

Her mother answered on the fifth ring and Ana wasted no time in getting to the point. 'We're not engaged,' she said. 'No matter what you heard during the press conference. Casimir was mistaken.'

'He tried to force your hand?' her mother asked sharply.

'No.' *Yes.* 'I gave him mixed messages and maybe slept with him again. Marriage came up as an option, a possibility, nothing more. He needs a wife and an heir. I'm a convenient option.' She tried to keep her voice steady as she spoke. 'I said no.'

Her mother said nothing.

'He wants us to remain in Byzenmaach,' Ana said next. 'He's very security-conscious.'

'And I know why,' her mother said. 'I made it my business to find out.'

'What else did you find out?' Never underestimate her mother's talent for gathering information.

'That he has his work cut out for him. His father divided a nation.'

'He knows that,' Ana said. 'You saw the press conference? What did you think of it?'

'I thought the water plans for the region were visionary, his olive branch to the rebels on his northern borders was reckless, and his family history tragic. His protectiveness when it came to you and Sophia made me weep with both joy and fear, for he has shown his weakness.'

'He doesn't want me to go back to Geneva,' said Ana.

'Neither do I. The damage is done. Stay where he can protect you.'

'He's offered me the dower house on the palace grounds.'

'Good. I hope there's room for visitors,' her mother said.

'There's room for a football team.' Ana stopped pacing and leaned back against the wall instead, and to hell with the gilded wallpaper. If it rubbed off, it rubbed off. Walls were meant for leaning on. 'Mama, he's a good man. He's trying with me and Sophia. He wants us around. I have a ring in my pocket that he wants me to put on my finger and it'd be easy, so easy, just to do it and become part of the royal machinery that surrounds him, with all the protection it affords. I said no.' She closed her eyes and thumped her head gently against the wall.

'What's stopping you?' Her mother's voice soothed, even as it demanded answers.

'He doesn't love me. I'm just convenient. A righting of wrongs and a means to an end.'

'And you've slept with him,' her mother said.

Ana sighed. 'Resistance is non-existent. He wants, I oblige, and we both win.'

'But you still said no to his proposal.'

Ana thumped her head against the wall again. Gently, but still… 'I could love him. Easily.' In a heartbeat, assuming she didn't already. 'I could be happy here. Sophia would have a father. There would be more children. I could keep working as a translator and keep that side of me functioning. I'm interested in Casimir's plans for Byzenmaach and I'm not politically naïve. I could be of use here.'

'I'm listening,' said her mother, and that was another thing she did very, very well.

'But he doesn't love me, Mama, and I don't know if he ever will. And I think if I married him and he never grew to love me, I would break. I don't want to break.'

Not again.

'I'm going to conquer this world,' she continued. 'I'm going to carve out a place in it and maybe one day…'

She took a deep breath and exposed her deepest desire. 'Maybe one day I'll stand at Casimir's side, secure in the knowledge that he loves me as dearly as I love him. But not today.'

'That's my girl,' her mother said.

Six hours later, Casimir walked into his bedchamber at the winter fortress and caught his breath at the sight before him. Soft lamps lit the drinks on the sideboard. Beside them sat a plate of misshapen chocolate chip cookies and a haphazard posy of flowers. The posy was an odd mixture of clover leaves, violets, crooked twigs and pretty leaves that a small girl might collect in her hand. A note sat next to the posy, with an arrow pointing towards the cookies. *For my king*, it said. *Love from Sophia*, and he felt a tiny hand reach for his heart and take hold.

An envelope sat beside it, not quite flat, and he knew what it was before he reached for it. His grandmother's ring fell out into his hand, but it wasn't the ring he was interested in. She'd left him a note, and his hands shook as he opened the folded paper.

Not yet. I don't want either of us to make a mistake. As for your unification speech for Byzenmaach, it took my breath away with its vision and generosity towards old foes.

For your protective introduction of Sophia and of me, I can only say thank you.

Sleep well, Casimir. I'll see you in the morning.

She wouldn't wear his ring, but nor had she left him. That was something.

CHAPTER TEN

THREE DAYS LATER Ana was quietly going round the twist. She had plenty to do; that wasn't the problem. Arrange for her and Sophia's belongings to be sent from Geneva to the dower house. Acquire clothes for them both that they could wear on their first official outing with Casimir. Try and arrange schooling for Sophia, and wasn't that an endeavour of gigantic proportions. Most of all she got to watch an increasingly stern Casimir as he left every morning for the capital and returned every evening with a bleak gaze and a weary smile.

The factions to the north hadn't responded to his invitations yet.

Rudolpho counselled patience but Casimir didn't want to hear it.

Lor simply shook her head and refused to talk about it.

When it came to the matter of schooling for Sophia, Ana sought Lor's counsel above all others. The older woman knew things and had endless patience for Ana's questions.

'Am I really asking the impossible by wanting Sophia to go to school?' Ana asked as they sat at the computer and studied the list of schools Ana's new secretary had sent through. 'What do royal children normally do?'

'There's no hard and fast rule.'

'Casimir said he had tutors.'

Lor nodded. 'Even before the tragedies he rarely mixed with other children. Only other royal children who came visiting. Augustus and Moriana. Theo of Liesendaach—and what a tearaway that one was. Valentine of Thallasia and his sister—those two were designed to break hearts, I've never seen more beautiful children. They were Casimir's friends. He keeps them close.'

'I'm getting that.' Three of them were kings in their own right and fighting just as hard for regional reform as Casimir. 'Did they go to school or did they have tutors too?'

'Augustus and Moriana went to school. Theo too.' Lor frowned. 'Valentine and Amira, no. They had tutors.'

'What do you think I should do when it comes to schooling Sophia?'

'I think she's a gregarious girl who needs to go to school, make friends and have as normal an upbringing as possible, under the circumstances.'

That was what Ana's mother had said too. 'My daughter is down in the aviary with Tomas, learning what to feed orphaned baby birds. I have no doubt that half a wolfhound pack is sitting at her feet and when she's finished with the birds I guarantee she'll con someone to take her to visit the little pink saddle and the little Arabian mare that have miraculously appeared in the stables. I think the normal upbringing ship has sailed.'

Lor snorted. 'You could always ask Casimir about the saddle. And the pony.'

'I would if I ever saw him before bedtime.' And there was the crux of the problem. 'Does he always work this hard? Because, honestly, Lor, there should be two of him.'

'It's a difficult time.' Lor shrugged and pulled away from the computer, standing and reaching for the shawl she'd slung over the back of her chair upon entering Ana's office—a word that didn't quite fit the airy parlour with the view of the walled gardens and beyond that the grassy plains and then the mountains. 'Casimir feels he has something to prove. Something to fix. You're welcome to try telling him he doesn't.'

'Yeah, thanks. Trouble is, I like what he's trying to do. I think it shows courage, vision and strength. I want him to succeed.' Every day when she saw what he was aiming to do and the challenges he faced she wanted that for him. She stood abruptly. 'I'm going for a walk to try and clear my head. I might even make school decisions while I'm at it.'

'Take your coat and don't wander far,' warned Lor. 'There's a front coming in from the west. The weather will turn.'

'I'll take Sophia too. We may not make it past the stables,' Ana replied, although maybe she'd get punchy and venture beyond the castle walls.

She found Sophia at the falconry with Tomas and watched for a while as they finished tending the baby birds. Tomas had infinite patience, with both the birds and her daughter, and if every now and then his smile hinted at painful memories he couldn't quite hide, no one spoke of it.

Tomas told her about the selection of weatherproof coats at the stables, behind the tack-room door, and frowned down at Sophia before finally deciding that her little pink parka and ankle boots were okay.

Sophia needed new clothes more suited to her new life; Ana had already received that memo. They were on their way.

The new pony's name was Duchess, Sophia informed her. Duchess liked carrots, apples, a heated stall and little girls. Sophia knew all the horses in the stalls—of course she did. Names *and* temperaments. Which horses would hang their heads over the doors to be petted and which bad-tempered beasts to stay away from.

They'd make a stateswoman out of her daughter yet.

Sophia was happy here. With Lor and Silas at her beck and call, and all the animals. Sophia didn't care about her current lack of schooling at all. She was learning more than she ever had. Some things *were* working out just fine.

They slipped outside the stable doors and beyond the fortress walls in search of wildflowers, and started along the bridle path towards the mountains. They'd done it before. Just them, the ground underfoot and the sky. The security guards could see them from the fortress walls and were content to give them the illusion of freedom. She and Sophia would walk the fields for a while and then return. No harm done.

A carefree hour later, somewhere on a bridle path, the weather closed in around them. One minute the sun was shining and the next minute clouds were rolling in and bringing a heavy mist with them.

Ana turned back immediately, Sophia's hand in hers and Lor's warning in mind, but it was too late. The air was turning to soup and Ana could no longer see six feet in front of her. They'd been able to see the fortress a minute ago and they were still on the track. Nothing to worry about. They couldn't be more than a kilometre or two away.

'What is this?' asked Sophia, waving her hand through the mist.

'It's a cloud, and we're in it. I think it came over the mountain and fell on us.'

'Will it float away again?'

'Yes.' *When?* being the pertinent question. 'Meanwhile—' she looked at the track, only to find it disappearing as she spoke '—we sit.'

'And then what?' asked Sophia dubiously.

'We sing.' And hope someone came for them or the enveloping fog moved on so that they could see their way home again. Ana wasn't picky. Either one would do.

Casimir had got into the habit of finding Ana and Sophia whenever he returned to the fortress. The mere sight of them was usually enough to quiet the demon inside him that wanted to lock them away and keep them safe.

He still hadn't heard from the tribespeople to the north. Four days since his speech; Rudolpho counselled patience and said they'd have to speak amongst themselves before replying, and Theo had counselled similarly. And still he felt as if his skin were slipping his body half the time and that his people were beginning to wonder whether he really could deliver on this grand plan he'd offered them.

He needed to appear in public with Ana and Sophia soon, and the security risks ate at him, reminding him that grand plans had been so much easier to create when he hadn't had anything to lose.

Schools. Heaven help him, he was going to send his daughter to school; it was a life she knew and a world he was wholly unaccustomed to. He'd spent the afternoon in crisis talks with Rudolpho.

Over schools.

Ana would doubtless spend a good portion of the night trying to reassure him that schooling was a perfectly normal endeavour for a child and that his daughter would fit in just fine.

He wanted her to fit in.

But schools and the security risks that went with them. Heaven help him.

Ana and Sophia weren't in Lor's kitchen and he didn't think they'd be anywhere in the garden. His pilot had barely been able to land the helicopter, given the limited visibility. Only the latest navigation system had allowed them down safely, and even then his pilot had been cursing.

They weren't in the Queen's quarters or the sunroom Ana had claimed as her office.

They weren't in the bathhouse.

They weren't in the library.

Ten minutes later he got the sinking feeling they weren't in the fortress at all, especially once Lor told him Ana had been going to take Sophia for walk.

By the time his guards had checked the aviary, the stables, the gardens and every other outbuilding in existence, his unease was evident. Every last member of staff had been accounted for. Not a security guard or groundsman was missing.

Ana and Sophia were the only ones missing. 'Search the fortress again from top to bottom. Every room, every passageway, every goddamn cupboard!'

'They were going for a walk,' Lor said, and not for the first time, only not one of his guards had seen them venture beyond the walls.

'They were headed for the stables,' added Tomas.

'Which would be of help if they were still in the stables. Which they're *not*. Search the grounds again. *Now.*' People nodded and refused to catch his eye as they melted from sight.

He never roared. In all his years Casimir had never roared. Until now.

He wondered, with an increasing sense of being out

of control, whether he should release the wolfhounds.
The dogs would scent their trail. One would, at any rate.
The dog and his daughter were damn near inseparable.
'Where's Jelly?'

'In the kitchen with her puppies,' said Lor.

The big wolfhound was happy to see him and seemed
to know what he wanted when he put one of Sophia's
shoes to her nose. She led him to the stables and scratched
at the door that led to the bridle path, so he saddled the
big black stallion he usually rode while Tomas saddled
a nearby mare.

Members of his security team were already fanning
out beyond the walls, although what good they were
if they could let a six-year-old girl and her mother *slip
through their fingers…*

'I've seen them follow the bridle path before,' Tomas
said in a voice tight with worry as they followed the loping wolfhound out and onto the bridle path. 'Following
butterflies. Picking flowers. They do that.'

That was all Claudia had been doing too, when they'd
taken her. She'd been inside the garden walls and sup-
posedly well protected.

And then she'd been gone.

'I stirred up the northerners.' Out here, with a man
he'd known since childhood, Casimir could finally voice
his greatest fear. 'I've been pushing them.'

'No.' This time his falconer's voice came firm and
hard. 'You're giving them a chance to sit at the negotiating table again. They won't refuse that. They won't make
old mistakes again.'

'You don't know that. *I* don't know that.'

'I know there are no strangers about. There's no one
lying in wait for the opportunity to take Sophia and Ana
away from you. I flew falcons today. Falcons trained

to circle at the presence of humans. *They* would have known.'

'You trust falcons?'

'More than I trust people,' said Tomas.

They headed in the direction of the mountain pass, the dog confident in her direction. This was the bridle path that wove through the outer pastures before joining the road. A tempting walk for a woman and child. He hoped.

He called for them at intervals, Ana's name, and then Sophia's, and he could hear the fear in his voice and so smothered it with anger.

No one had taken them. He *had* to believe that.

History could not repeat itself.

They were just lost.

They were sitting on a rock beside the bridle path, singing, when he and Tomas finally reached them. Jelly had led them straight to them. He could give the dog a medal later. Name a valley after her. He reined the stallion in and slid to the ground, his fury barely contained.

'See?' Ana said by way of greeting. 'I told you someone would find us if we sang.'

'Do you have any idea how many people are looking for you?' he began.

'Er—'

'Everyone! Everyone is looking for you.'

'We just—'

'Don't you dare say you went for a walk.'

'Not even if it's the truth?'

'Where is your guide?'

'I didn't think—'

'Indeed you did *not*.'

Ana's beautiful, beloved features took on a mutinous slant.

'We weren't going far. We can see the fortress from here!'

'Oh, you can, can you?' he snarled, heavy on the sarcasm. 'Because no one at the fortress can see *you*.'

'Well, we could,' said Ana. 'And when we couldn't we sat and waited and here you are.' She tried a tentative smile and lit Casimir's fury to new heights. 'No harm done.'

'You don't know these mountains,' he said.

'We've been gone twenty minutes.'

'Do you even wear at watch?' He couldn't see one.

'An hour at the most,' she amended.

An hour too long. 'You could have been killed. Or taken.' Or worse.

'Now you're projecting.'

'I have the right. *Get up.*'

Sophia was already up, staring at the furious man in front of her with wide eyes. He crouched down and ran a hand through his hair. He was scaring them; he knew he was. 'Hey,' he said gruffly. 'I was worried about you.'

'Me too,' Sophia whispered, and then stepped closer and put cold hands to his cheeks as she studied his face. 'Are you crying?'

'It's just moisture from the clouds.' The hell it was. 'Jelly found you,' he said and gathered her close and held tight. This child. How had she found her way into his heart so fast? 'And my horse is going to take you home.'

Her arms tightened around his neck. 'That's the cranky horse. Tomas said we couldn't ride him.'

'Not alone, no.' Tomas was right. 'You can ride with Tomas.' He spared a glance for the man who'd ridden alongside him.

'Maman has to come too.'

'She can ride with me.' He stood, with Sophia still

clinging to him, and stared at the woman who could fill his heart with terror as easily as she could make it soar. 'I thought I'd lost you.'

She shook her head and her eyes filled with tears. 'No.'

'We were coming back,' his little girl said, with her arms tightly wrapped around his neck. 'We were always coming back to you. We just couldn't see the way.'

A very subdued Ana rode back to the fortress behind Casimir. Sophia rode with Tomas, who had not long ago sounded a hunting horn. A message to those back at the fortress, signalling that Ana and Sophia had been found. Sophia had wanted him to sound the horn again but Tomas had refused her. To sound the horn again and again would be a call to arms, Tomas had told them.

This place...

It didn't take long for them to reach the stables. The fog was still rolling in but both Cas and Tomas appeared to have a homing instinct and so did the dog.

They were still on horseback when they slipped through the door and entered the stables. The doors closed behind them with an emphatic thud and the number of people waiting for them far exceeded the number of horses.

He really had had everyone out looking for them.

'I'm very sorry,' she murmured as she dismounted. 'I should have been more observant about the weather.'

Casimir's lips tightened. He didn't say a word, merely handed the horse to a groomsman.

'I should have stayed closer to home and heeded Lor's warning,' she said next, as Lor took Sophia from Tomas and hugged her close. Tomas wouldn't look at her, or at anyone else for that matter. The falconer looked pallid and drawn, as if he'd aged twenty years since she'd seen him last.

As for Casimir, he was already striding from the stables.

No one spoke. Not one person, until Tomas finally looked at her. 'The northerners aren't co-operating. He thought they'd taken you.'

Oh.

Oh.

She looked to Tomas with his white face and Lor with her pinched lips and to her daughter, who was in good hands. 'Sophia needs a bath,' she said, because of course that made sense. And then she turned and began to run towards her king.

She caught up with him at the bottom of the stairs that led to the landing overlooking the garden. He didn't slow down and she struggled to keep up, taking two steps at a time and silently cursing the sheer number of them.

'I should have told someone which way I was going,' she said when they reached the landing.

'You should have taken a guide,' he said in a tone made all the more menacing by its mildness.

'I wasn't thinking.' Too distracted by all the changes in her world to note the change of weather coming in, never mind that she'd been warned. She hadn't known what that warning *meant*. It hadn't meant to her what it meant to the people who lived here. 'I'm sorry for all the concern I caused. I know better now. It won't happen again.'

'You're right; it won't. Your chances of going anywhere ever again without a full security detail on your tail are non-existent.'

'That seems a little…extreme.' There was contrition and then there was total loss of privacy.

'You think so? I don't think so,' he said.

He looked to be heading to the library, so she followed

him and watched as he poured a drink from the decanter on the sideboard. The liquid glowed amber in the soft lamplight and he knocked it back hard and poured another. That went the same way as the first and his hand trembled.

'It won't happen again,' she said. 'No need to put people on me twenty-four hours a day. That won't be necessary. I'll be more mindful. Cas—'

'This would go so much better,' he said, 'if you didn't talk.'

She waited, but he didn't fill the silence. For a very long time she stood there while he paced and glowered and looked anywhere but at her.

'This would go so much better if you *did* talk,' she said finally. 'Casimir, I'm still here. I'm right here. And I'm listening.'

He didn't know where to begin. He couldn't find a way to cut through the immobilising fear of losing her and speak to the heart of things. Anger ruled his movements, stiff and fierce, and he couldn't look at her for fear of losing his way.

'I brought you into this,' he began. 'I know I shouldn't have but I did it anyway and if you die because of me, because of dangers I haven't made clear or because some political outsiders want revenge on me, that's on me.'

'How can you say you brought me—?'

'Damned if I brought you here to die. Don't you chase that road. Don't you do that to me!'

There it lay. His fear of losing everyone he loved, bright and shiny and finally spoken. Time to walk away now, before anger and fear got him saying all sorts of things he shouldn't, but he couldn't make himself move.

'Don't you leave me.'

He tried to turn away but she was right there beside him, raising her hand to his cheek and not to strike him but to cup it, and he closed his eyes at the sweetness.

'This fear isn't real,' she murmured fiercely. 'It's one of your shadows. Casimir, look at me.'

He couldn't. He couldn't do this love thing. 'I need you to be more careful,' he managed.

'I can be. That's what I'm telling you.' She kissed him, soothed him.

He didn't want to love this hard. He hated it. That was the biggest difference between them. She *wanted* to love wholeheartedly.

He took her lips more roughly than she'd taken his; he let passion and fear mix and burn white. When she twined her arms around his neck, he backed her against the wall and tried not to let his hunger get the better of him. He pushed her hair to one side and buried his face in her neck, tasting, trailing, finding her pulse-point with his tongue and letting its rapid beat chase away the lingering flavour of death. *Not this time. Not dead.*

Take a man who'd lost everyone he'd ever cared about and give him a family and then threaten to take it away and see how he fared.

'I'm right here,' she said quietly. 'I believe in what you're doing. What you're fighting for. I'm right here beside you, and I am not afraid to be.' She fisted her hand in his hair, licked his lips open and cut off his breath. They were both breathing hard when she released him. 'Can we have make-up sex now?'

'Yes.' Of all the things she'd asked of him, that one he could do.

CHAPTER ELEVEN

To say that security got tighter after that would be an understatement. When Cas wasn't with her—and he was with her far more than he'd ever been—Tomas would magically appear, or Silas would show up, or Lor's niece, who was now Sophia's nanny, would drop by. Ana had yet to see a roster but dammit they had one and the purpose of that roster was to make sure that Ana was never alone. She'd stake her life on it.

The sooner she made her way to the dower house and eked out some small semblance of privacy the better.

It was a week after the incident with the fog, as she preferred to call it, and the dower house wasn't ready yet and Sophia's schooling still hadn't been organised and Cas had flown to the capital to meet with Augustus.

Two weeks ago she'd been in Geneva, going about her business. These days she was thoroughly embroiled in Byzenmaach politics. If she wasn't in the library reading up on the history of the region, she was at Rudolpho to feed her more reports. She'd taken extended leave from her work for the UN.

Her call, and no one else's. There was too much to come up to speed on here.

The majority of Byzenmaach's people had rallied behind Casimir and his plans, but the northerners had yet to reveal their intentions.

And then Sophia skidded into the room, her eyes wide and her cheeks red. 'Tomas says you have to come to the tower,' she said.

'Why? Are you flying falcons today?'

'Yes, and the riders are coming.' Sophia's excitement was evident. 'A lady and a man and they're armed and Tomas is all upset and you have to come *now*.'

'Armed how?'

'They have *wolfhounds*.'

'Oh.' This world… 'Better get Silas too.'

'He's already there,' said Sophia.

Many, many grey stone steps later, Ana stood on the battlements and gazed out across the plains towards the mountain pass. Two riders were approaching, two wolfhounds, two horses. And Tomas was in a right state.

He'd flown a falcon upon their approach, he told her. A falcon with a strip of royal purple cloth around one leg instead of the traditional leather jesses. He'd flown the cloth because it was a welcome, of sorts. A message— for those who could understand it—that they were now under the king's personal protection.

'Okay. So far so good,' Ana said when the usually taciturn Tomas stopped for breath. She looked to Silas for direction but he offered no guidance. 'So the falcon flew a piece of purple cloth as a welcome. What happened next?'

'That woman got off her horse, pulled a gauntlet from her saddlebag and called my bird to her hand,' Tomas said. 'The bird now flies a white strip of cloth and *two* strips of purple. She's saying that royalty is coming, in peace.' Tomas paced, his eyes a little wild. 'It was only whimsy that made me fly the cloth. Superstition. An old, old custom. And then she had the audacity to call *my* bird straight out of the sky. Using *my* signals.'

Tomas the falconer was the calmest man Ana knew.

Except for now.

'So...she's a falconer too?'

'He thinks it's Claudia,' Silas said calmly, his eyes never leaving Tomas's face.

'I didn't *say* that,' said Tomas.

'But you think it.' The older man was giving the falconer no quarter.

'Just to be clear, you're talking Claudia as in Casimir's dead sister?' Ana looked from one man to the other. 'You're serious.'

'We never got her body back,' Tomas said stubbornly.

'We got some of it back,' said Silas.

'Okay,' Ana said hurriedly. 'Six-year-old girl on the battlements. Listening.'

Tomas flushed red. Silas shut his eyes and shook his head.

'Is there any way we can get a look at the woman's face?' she asked, and Tomas handed her a set of binoculars.

'She's wearing traditional headdress. Only part of her face is showing,' he said. 'It could be her. It could be anyone.'

'But you think it's her,' said Ana.

'I don't *know*.' Tomas turned away and swore profusely, and that was another thing he never did—at least not in front of Ana and Sophia. '*She* knew about the coloured cloth instead of jesses and what they meant. It's in one of the royal falconry journals and I read that section aloud to her one day when she was helping me nurse a hawk with a broken wing. She was good with the birds. They trusted her. She knew all the call signals.'

'Why would she stay away all these years, only to return now?' asked Silas.

'Because the father who left her to rot is dead, her brother is whole and happy, Byzenmaach is moving forward and she wants to come home?' snapped Tomas. 'How should I know?'

'But you think it's her,' said Ana. 'Again, just to be clear.'

'Yes.' The word sounded as if it had been dragged from Tomas's soul.

'Then we need to tell Cas.'

'And say what?' Tomas started pacing again. 'You would have me talk of colours and hawks and then tell him I think his sister's alive? Do I tell him I can feel her on the wind, like a storm coming in? He'll think me mad. *I* think I'm mad.'

'They're heading for the bridle path,' Silas said suddenly.

'They would have heard about it in the village,' Tomas replied.

'They're taking the *old* bridle path,' Silas said, and there was a whole lot of silence after that.

'Is there another not dead dead person coming?' asked Sophia.

Ana really didn't want to say *maybe* in answer to that question. But she did. 'Maybe.'

Everyone watched the two riders and their hounds accelerate into a loping canter. 'How long before they get here?' she asked.

'Two hours, if they keep to the pace they're going,' said Silas.

'And if they push it?'

'Half that.'

* * *

Casmir sat with Augustus and a room full of advisors, trying to debate the merits of Augustus approaching the rebels to the north when an aide summoned Rudolpho from the room. That wasn't so strange in itself, but the fact that Rudolpho returned with a frown, holding a phone that he held out to Casimir was.

'Ana,' the older man said, and Casimir immediately feared the worst. Why had Rudolpho brought the phone into the meeting? Why hadn't he called Casimir out of the room to take the call? There was a protocol for the way phone calls were handled. And his head advisor wasn't following it.

He took the phone and headed for the door. 'What is it?' he asked.

'Two riders are approaching by horseback,' Ana said. 'Silas thinks they're an envoy from the north and Tomas thinks he knows one of them. You need to be here within the hour to greet them.'

'And you and Sophia need to *not* be there. Start packing.'

'Not on your life,' she said.

'You will stay away from them.' He could feel his temper rising.

'That I can do. Until you get here and then we'll see. Rudolpho says you're in an important meeting.'

'I've just stepped out.' He closed the door behind him.

'Are you alone?'

'Yes.'

'Tomas says you can fire him if he's wrong. Personally, I don't think you'll need to. He'll probably jump off a cliff if he's wrong.'

'Ana, what is it?'

'One of the envoy is a woman and there's no easy way to say this so I'm just going to say it. Tomas thinks it's Claudia.'

Forty-seven minutes later, Casimir landed in the court-yard of the winter fortress. His security team had run the faces of the riders through recognition software and the elder male had been identified as a statesman for the mountain tribes to the north. No surprises there. The woman remained unidentified but Casimir had seen the picture, black and white and grainy as it was, and Tomas could be forgiven for thinking it was her. If it wasn't her—if they'd deliberately chosen a negotiator who re-sembled his dead sister...

If they'd done that he would be hard pressed to ne-gotiate at all.

'Any more information?' he asked as he fell into step alongside Silas and headed towards the door.

'They're ten minutes out, Tomas can barely speak and Sophia is wearing her best dress and shiniest shoes be-cause her dead aunt's coming to town.'

Oh, dear God.

'Breathe,' said Silas.

'Sophia's secure?'

'In the playroom, under guard.'

'And Anastasia?'

'On the battlements with Tomas.'

Then that was where he wanted to be. He adjusted course and when he got there and Ana smiled at him he felt his world settle again into something he had a hope of controlling. He clasped Tomas's arm next and drew his childhood playmate into an embrace.

'Hell of a day,' he said. 'Let's go find out who she is.'

'They're stopping,' said Ana, and it was true. Less

than five hundred metres from the walls the two riders had stopped to dismount. The man held out his arms and slowly turned in a circle and then shed his riding cloak and then his outer tunic. He heaped them on the ground and a scimitar followed. The rifle at his back was added to the pile. A sheathed knife at his ankle got thrown on top of that. The woman did the same with her weapons, up to and including the long slender pencil-like rods in her hair.

'Hidden knives,' said Tomas.

'Well, at least she's getting rid of them. I'm sure she'll feel lighter,' said Ana, responding to Casimir's dark amusement with a shrug and open hands.

The woman's dark hair was plaited and fell to her waist. Her features were proud and her movements graceful. Casimir stared hard and tried to fit the face of a child onto the face of the woman who rode, but it was no use. Claudia or not, time had moved on and she was not the sister he remembered.

They left their belongings in two neat heaps and remounted their horses, their pace sedate as they continued their approach.

'Send someone out to pick up their belongings and tell the snipers to stand down,' he told Silas.

'Snipers?' Ana looked aghast.

'Precaution.' Time to get to the stables. 'Coming?'

'You really need to stop making that sound like a command,' she said.

'King,' he countered, and took her hand so that she could feel its tremble and know he was holding onto his composure by a thread and that he needed her close.

'I don't suppose there's a rule book for this meeting?' she asked. 'Protocol to follow? Curtseys to make?'

'No. But if I falter, step in.'

'I will. But you won't falter.' Her quiet certainty buoyed him. This was what it was like to have someone in your corner, he thought. This was what it felt like to be the recipient of someone else's strength.

He felt the warmth of it and finally, willingly, let the last of his defences fall. He wanted this with all his heart. This world in which he loved hard and was loved just as hard in return.

'I love you,' he said in Russian. 'So much. I understand now, what it feels like to stand beside the woman I love and feel loved in return. You were right. There is no place I'd rather be.'

She stumbled and would have teetered but for her hand in his.

'You pick your times,' she muttered, but her hand tightened in his. 'I can't believe that out of all the opportunities you've had of late, you're telling me this now.'

The stables weren't like any other stables Ana had ever seen. Twenty stalls capable of holding three or four horses apiece ran either side of a large central square. The square was covered in sawdust and the stable hands kept it immaculate. Huge wooden doors stood open at both ends of the square. Doors strong enough to hold invaders out more than horses in.

Ana waited alongside Cas, with Tomas on her other flank. A dozen more security people stood dotted around, all of them armed.

The male rider was the first to dismount, doing so before he reached the doors and walking his horse in. His gaze fixed on Casimir as he let his horse's reins drop and he stepped forward. 'Your Majesty,' he said. 'It's been a long time.'

Casimir nodded. 'Welcome, Lord Ildris. Who's your companion?'

Lord Ildris waited a beat before speaking, as if choosing his words with the utmost care. 'A future for a future,' he offered quietly. 'She's the negotiator you requested and speaks for the people of the north and for herself.'

The woman had dismounted but her eyes remained lowered. She strode into the stables, swift and sure, and the horse and dogs followed. Whoever she was, she didn't lack confidence. And then she raised her gaze and her eyes said it all.

The woman had eyes the same shape and colour as Casimir's. The same eyes as Sophia. The eyes of the royal family of Byzenmaach.

'Hello Casimir,' she said and her gaze flickered sideways for a moment. 'Tomas. You're the falconer here now?'

'Yes,' said Ana when Tomas appeared incapable of speech. 'He is.'

The woman smiled gently. 'I thought so.' And then her gaze returned to Casimir and her expression grew a whole lot more complex. 'Brother. It's been a long time.'

Cas too seemed incapable of movement or speech. 'Guess she's not *dead*, dead either,' Ana muttered in Russian because he needed a push and was fluent in the language and boy were they going to have words about *that* later. 'Welcome her home.'

And then Cas was striding across the sawdust and pulling his sister into an embrace that left no room for air, and if anyone could have ever doubted his love for his sister, the depth of his loss or the extent of his joy at seeing her alive, they couldn't possibly doubt it now because it was written all over his face.

'Lord Ildris,' Ana said, forcing the man's attention.

'You must be weary after your travels. We have a bath-house here I think you'll like. And refreshments and rooms available for your use. Come.' She was beginning to understand why Casimir used that word a lot. 'Let us leave others to their reunion, shall we? We shall meet up with them again for a meal soon enough.'

She waited until he'd joined her and then headed for the fortress. The walk would take several minutes. They could chat along the way. She could wring his neck.

The four-man security detail surrounding them probably wouldn't stop her.

'I hear you have a daughter,' Lord Ildris said when they were halfway through the gardens.

'Yes, and I do hope you like wolfhound puppies because we currently have eight of them.'

'I too keep wolfhounds,' he replied easily. 'Perhaps we can arrange an exchange.'

'Exchanges do seem to be your forte.' He could take that any way he liked. She waited until they'd reached the steps that led from the garden to the patio before mounting her next offensive. 'Why now?' she asked. 'After all these years, why return her now?'

'You disapprove?'

'I'm new around here. I barely know which way is up. But I do question the motives of a man who would remove a child from her family only to produce her again twenty years later.'

'I'm afraid that's a question for Claudia to answer.'

'Are you her lover?'

'No!' His eyes snapped ice. 'Claudia has not been misused by us. Not as a child. Not as a woman. Which is more than I can say for her own family. She stayed with us because she wanted to stay and returns of her own free will. That is all I have to say on the matter.'

Protective. How very interesting.

She led him to a suite of rooms that were often used by various aides who overnighted at the fortress and opened the door for him. 'Do you or Claudia have any dietary requirements I should know about? I'd hate to poison you by accident.'

'I have no special dietary requirements and neither does Claudia.'

'Excellent. We dine at seven. I'd suggest a tour of the aviaries beforehand but my falconer's currently having a meltdown at the unexpected arrival of his long-lost childhood friend. Perhaps next time.'

'Of course,' he said. 'May I be permitted to congratulate you on your engagement?'

'Sure,' she said. 'Go right ahead.'

'A woman of humour is a rare asset for a king,' he said. 'Ms Douglas, mother of the young duchess of Sanesch, future consort to the king of Byzenmaach, it is my pleasure to make your acquaintance.'

And she'd thought the UN was a diplomatic circus. 'Rest well, Lord Ildris. The belongings you parted with earlier will be brought to your room. Some of them, at any rate. The rest will be held in safe keeping until your departure. We'll see you at dinner.'

Later, much later that evening, long after dinner had been served and dessert had been eaten, Ana stood in Casimir's bedroom and waited for him to start shedding his clothes.

'So,' he said, 'Claudia's alive.' He looked a little lost, a little low. He'd walked his sister to her guest room and clearly had plenty on his mind.

'She likes Sophia.' Casimir's sister had won a lot of ground with her unforced attention for the wide-eyed little girl with the ruby-red shoes and the blue eggshell that simply had to come from a dragon.

'Yes.' He loosened his tie. 'I asked her why she stayed away all these years.'

'Oh.' He'd speak when he was ready, or not at all.

'She said she had the opportunity to return, several times over, but that she would not go where she wasn't wanted. She said my father renounced her. That he thought she was not his and that my mother had had an affair.'

'With those eyes?' Because, seriously, if ever there was an inherited trait...

'An affair with my uncle, who had the eyes. He died in a hunting accident in the mountains. Before Claudia was born.'

'So is he *dead*, dead, or likely to arrive any minute?'

Casimir's eyes warmed just for her. 'I love what you bring to my world.'

'You're welcome.' She had a new nightgown she wanted to bring to his world too. It was ivory silk with amber ribbon bows, but now was probably not the time.

'I was three years old at the time, but I'm going to say that my uncle is dead. By all accounts his body came down from the mountain after the accident. We buried him.'

Cas began to remove his cufflinks, but he wasn't undressing to please her. His thoughts were still firmly lodged in the past. 'Claudia believes my father found out about my mother's affair and had my uncle killed. My father then claimed Claudia as his own, but changed his tune when she was kidnapped. He didn't care what her captors did with her. And my mother knew why and killed herself. It makes sense.'

Maniacal sense.

'Lord Ildris's wife took Claudia in. When she was ten they told her everything and asked if she wanted to return to the palace. She didn't. At eighteen, they asked again if Claudia wanted to return.'

'And she didn't,' Ana said quietly.

'All these years she let me think she was dead and that it was somehow my fault. I blamed myself for her death and for my mother's death and no one ever told me I was wrong to do so,' he said roughly. 'I want to be angry with all of them, and with Claudia for letting me think she was dead, but I can't. Claudia was a pawn. A child who thought no one wanted her, and when she was offered a way out she took it. Her allegiance now is to the north. Not to me.'

'And yet she returns to you, flying royal colours. Don't write her allegiances off so easily, Casimir. Wait and see. Because it seems to me you may both want the same thing. A new beginning.'

Casimir said nothing.

'Does she want to be acknowledged as your sister or your half-sister?'

'I don't know.' He rubbed at the royal ring he wore. 'We never got that far in conversation.'

'What would *you* prefer? The lie or the truth?'

He shrugged. 'Me the man or me the monarch?'

'This is our bedchamber.' Okay, *his* bedchamber, but she slept here too these days. 'Out there, at the dinner table tonight, I sat with the king in front of guests of unknown influence and responded accordingly. When we're in here I'm speaking to the man. I prefer the man. I'm really not here for the figurehead.'

The man smiled crookedly. 'The identity of Claudia's father doesn't change my feelings for her or my joy at knowing she's alive and well. She's my sister. My family. Mine to love. I don't do things by halves.'

He certainly did not. Which reminded her of his words on the battlements and that she had her own bone to pick with him.

'So,' she said mildly because she'd been patient with him all evening. She'd been patient with everyone all evening. Clearly she had the patience of a *saint*. 'You speak Russian.'

'Ah,' he said. 'Yes.'

'You let *me* speak Russian up by the watch tower.' His tie came off and then his snowy white shirt. The view of the valleys and crests of his chest was impressive but she refused to be distracted by pleasures of the flesh.

'In my defence, I really did just want to hear you speak the language. I even gave you a book to read from. You were the one who went off the page.'

'You said we had no secrets left.'

'And we don't,' he said as he unbuckled his belt.

'Trousers stay on,' she commanded. 'I'm not falling for that old trick ever again.'

'I'm very tired,' he said next.

'Coward.'

'And overwrought,' he continued doggedly. 'My sister just returned from the dead.'

'Say it again.'

'My sister just—oomph!'

Her shoe had connected with his crotch. Granted, it wasn't attached to her foot, but who needed a karate black belt when she had a good throwing arm and exceptionally good aim?

'That was below the belt,' he said.

'I have been very patient with you,' she began. 'I have put up with your autocratic ways and your tendency not to share your thoughts and feelings unless naked or pressed. I have given up my career and embraced a whole new world for you. I have born you a daughter. There is nothing I wouldn't do for you, and you know it. Now say it again.'

'I was going to have candles set out all around the room,' he said, but his eyes were alight with unholy appreciation. 'And jewellery, lots and lots of jewellery. A tiara.'

'I do like tiaras,' she said and picked up her other shoe and spun it until the stiletto heel faced him. 'I'm waiting.'

'Would you like to hear it in Russian or in French?'

She let fly with a grin and watched him double over when struck.

'King,' he wheezed. 'Crown jewels.'

'Still waiting,' she said.

'I love you.' He said it in French and she sniffed. It wasn't his mother tongue and it certainly wasn't hers.

'Again.'

'I love you.' He said it in Russian and that was much better. The words spoke to her heart but did they come from his?

'Again.'

'I love you. Beyond words, I will always love you.' He said it in his own tongue, and this time she believed him.

A deep peace settled in her heart. Claudia wasn't the only one who'd finally come home. 'I love you too. But you already knew that.'

'I'm really glad you're out of shoes,' he said. 'Nor am I as tired as I was before. I love endorphins.'

They were alone in his bedroom, and his eyes held a promise she was never going to get tired of seeing. 'Would you like me to give you something to do?' she asked.

'Yes.'

Playful Cas was back. The one who filled her heart to overflowing. 'Would you like to take the rest of your clothes off?'

'Why, yes.' Just a man, when all was said and done. A man who'd offered her his heart. 'I'd like that a lot.'

EPILOGUE

Two weeks later...

ANASTASIA DOUGLAS, FUTURE wife of King Casimir of Byzenmaach, was dressing for a ball. She wasn't doing it alone. A small would-be duchess oversaw the production, and Ana's future sister-in-law was getting dressed in the room too. Ana didn't know who was more nervous about the upcoming introduction to Byzenmaach society, her or Claudia, but there was comfort to be had from company and Ana wasn't about to say no to it.

Tailors had worked around the clock for a week in order to get the gowns ready to wear. Ana's creation was ivory silk with a beaded pearl bodice that was a slightly darker shade of ivory than the fabric. The gown was backless and the pearls curved up and over her curves to wrap lovingly around her neck in a high collar. Her hair had been styled by experts and her pearl earrings were upstaged only by the delicate pearl and diamond strands woven through her hair. The only other piece of jewellery she wore was a ring on her engagement finger. It was big, it was pink, and it had once belonged to Casimir's grandmother. It was a statement of intent.

Within a year, Anastasia Douglas was going to marry

the man she loved and who loved her back with a thoroughness and intensity that left her breathless.

It was the first time she'd worn it.

'I don't know if I'm ever going to get used to the jewels,' she said. 'They're so…'

'I know.' Beside her, Claudia lifted her hands to the tiara that sat on her head. Ana was not allowed to wear a tiara until after she was married, according to Lor, but Claudia could, and had chosen one from the vault, and hadn't that been a visit to the royal vault worth remembering. They'd taken Sophia, the Lady Serah, Rudolpho and a pile of dresses and had vowed to make the king's chief advisor crack a smile.

He'd done more than that. When his pomp and ceremony had finally shattered and he'd finally smiled, he'd also walked away to try and hide the tears in his eyes. The Lady Serah had said to let him be. She'd said that laughter had been a long time coming to these halls and that while the change was welcome, some—who had lived a lifetime in the shadows—found it overwhelming.

They'd stopped teasing him after that, and he'd put his defences back together and returned, only to have Sophia begin an animated conversation with him about whether he preferred the rings on her fingers to the ones on her toes.

He'd told her the history of each and every one of them with a sly and wicked humour, and won himself three Rudolpho fans for life.

The gown Claudia had chosen for the evening was the shimmering colour of beaten bronze and the designers had made the most of her slender form. It had a full gauzy skirt, a herringbone corsetry bodice and was strapless. With it she wore a purple and white sash denoting that she was a member of the royal family of Byzenmaach. The cross that pinned her sash low on the waist was a gift from the north, announcing her allegiance to one of their orders as well. The glittering diamond tiara on Claudia's head had belonged to her mother and her diamond necklace and earrings had come from the royal collection. She too wore her hair swept up in a style wholly flattering.

Sophia, future duchess and self-proclaimed member of the Order of the Dragon, was not going to the ball. *She* wore a white cotton nightgown with lace around the edges and a long strand of hopefully not priceless pearls draped across her thin frame and tied at the hip like a sash. She was barefoot and tousle-haired and danced around them, already in attendance at her own imaginary ball.

'I have jewels for you too,' Sophia said and opened her fist to reveal two small, smooth pebbles of mottled green. 'They're dragon stones and there's one for each of you. You have to wear them close to your heart.'

'Thank you,' said Claudia as she took one of the offered pebbles and tucked it into her bodice. 'For courage.'

'You can keep it,' said Sophia.

'I will.'

Ana took the other pebble and tucked it into her bodice too. Her daughter was in danger of becoming seriously indulged. 'How do we look?'

'Like princesses.' Sophia twirled and the pearls twirled with her. 'Papa said he was going to dance with you all night long. Both of you.'

'We should clone him,' said Ana.

'I heard that,' said a voice at the doorway and there he stood, resplendent in white tie and weighed down with medals and a sash just like Claudia's.

'Pinch me,' Ana muttered to her soon-to-be sister-in-law. 'But not somewhere people will see the bruise.'

Claudia stepped closer, smiled angelically at her brother and obligingly pinched Ana on the ass. 'That what you wanted?'

'Perfect.' She really was here and he really was real. Because sometimes she could have sworn she was living a fairy tale. 'All good.'

'Are we ready?' asked Casimir.

Sophia eyed him narrowly. 'Do you have your dragon stone?'

'Right here.' He patted the general direction of his heart.

'What's keeping it there?' Claudia asked with the lift of an elegant eyebrow, and Ana could really grow to like this woman.

'Duct tape.'

'I love you,' Ana said, because he should be told this often. The more she told him the more he lit up like Christmas morning. It was a good look on him.

'You two go ahead,' Claudia said. 'I'll stay with Sophia while you greet your guests and then I'll make my big entrance a little later in the evening, when everybody's there to appreciate it.'

'But I need back-up,' Ana protested.

'He's right there,' Claudia said. 'Indulge me. Please. I want to read to my niece and then show her the secret room that overlooks the ballroom. I want to stand her on a chair and slide the viewing panel open so we can watch you two dance.'

Casimir smiled.

'You are putty in their hands,' Ana told him.

'I'm putty in your hands as well,' he said. 'And you're

wearing my ring.' He'd left it by her bedside table earlier that evening. There was a question in his eyes.

'I am.' And she intended to keep wearing it. 'What are your thoughts on a spring wedding?'

His smile widened. 'I'm all for it.'

'Gloves,' said Claudia, and Ana clicked her fingers. She'd forgotten about the gloves. They were snowy white and slid up past her elbows. 'But if I wear the gloves, people won't be able to see the ring.'

'Does it matter?' he murmured. 'I'll know it's there.'

'Now your tiara,' said Sophia.

'I don't have a tiara. Lor says— Oh!' Because suddenly there was a tiara dangling from Casimir's fingertips and it was delicate and whimsical and made from the finest of silver wire, diamonds and pearls.

'Wear it,' said Casimir. 'It's my gift to you. It's not from the vault.'

'Pinch me again,' said Ana when the tiara was in place and she stood facing the mirror.

'It's real. *You're* real,' said Claudia. 'And the king's waiting.'

Ana took his hand and walked with him to the ballroom, where Casimir began to introduce her to his guests. He never missed a person and Ana's smile never dimmed and she never missed a name.

'Do you think Claudia and Sophia are watching us yet?' she asked some time later as the musicians tuned their instruments and Casimir led her to the centre of the dance floor and swept her into his arms.

'Yes.'

Music filled the room and Casimir's smile softened. 'I love you.' This time he said it in Latin. 'I'm planning on saying it in every language that exists, including all of the non-verbal ones.'

'You're my fairy tale,' she said. 'And I'm not talking about all the trappings. Being with you is the fairy tale. Here at your side.'

She put one hand on his shoulder and her other hand in his.

And they danced.

* * * * *

SAME GREAT STORIES...
STYLISH NEW LOOK!

We're having a makeover!
From next month we'll still be bringing
you the very best romance from authors
you love, with a fabulous new look.

LET'S TALK
Romance

For exclusive extracts, competitions
and special offers, find us online:

- **f** facebook.com/millsandboon
- 📷 @millsandboonuk
- 🐦 @millsandboon

Or get in touch on 0844 844 1351*

For all the latest titles coming soon,
visit millsandboon.co.uk/nextmonth

Want even more
ROMANCE?

Join our bookclub today!

'Mills & Boon books, the perfect way to escape for an hour or so.'

Miss W. Dyer

'Excellent service, promptly delivered and very good subscription choices.'

Miss A. Pearson

'You get fantastic special offers and the chance to get books before they hit the shops'

Mrs V. Hall

Visit millsandbook.co.uk/Bookclub and save on brand new books.

MILLS & BOON